Sagebrush Satan

The priestess pointed at the three of them, her teeth bared, her face almost ugly with hate as she shrieked, "Kill them! Kill them!"

Without hesitation, the congregation moved to obey. The two burly men who'd held Cord's arms dove for their shotguns just as Cord was stepping off the altar. Toth swiveled toward them, firing both guns. Both men groaned as they crumpled to the ground, dead or close to it. In the meantime, the men in the congregation were fumbling under their robes for their guns.

"Kill them!" the priestess screamed. "In the name of Satan!"

Cord saw several guns swinging toward him. Immediately he dropped to the altar floor, tucked his shoulder and rolled toward the table where the victim lay. He could hear the bullets thudding into the wooden floor, following him only inches behind. Finally he bumped into the table, grabbed one of the shotguns and, holding it at waist level, popped up on the other side of the table. When he did, he was looking into the twin barrels of the other shotgun, now leveled into his face by the high priestess. It was braced against her shoulder, and one of her eyes was closed, the other peering down the sight.

She giggled, her lips twisted cruelly . . .

Also by Pike Bishop:

DIAMONDBACK

ATTENTION: SCHOOLS AND CORPORATIONS

PINNACLE Books are available at quantity discounts with bulk purchases for educational, business or special promotional use. For further details, please write to: SPECIAL SALES MANAGER, Pinnacle Books, Inc., 1430 Broadway, New York, NY 10018.

WRITE FOR OUR FREE CATALOG

If there is a Pinnacle Book you want—and you cannot find it locally—it is available from us simply by sending the title and price plus 75¢ to cover mailing and handling costs to:

        Pinnacle Books, Inc.
        Reader Service Department
        1430 Broadway
        New York, NY 10018

Please allow 6 weeks for delivery.

_____Check here if you want to receive our catalog regularly.

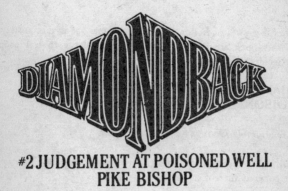

#2 JUDGEMENT AT POISONED WELL
PIKE BISHOP

PINNACLE BOOKS   NEW YORK

To Bob Irvine. A fine writer, a finer friend.

This is a work of fiction. All the characters and events portrayed in this book are fictional, and any resemblance to real people or incidents is purely coincidental.

DIAMONDBACK #2: JUDGEMENT AT POISONED WELL

Copyright © 1983 by Raymond Obstfeld.

All rights reserved, including the right to reproduce this book or portions thereof in any form.

An original Pinnacle Books edition, published for the first time anywhere.

First printing, September 1983

ISBN: 0-523-41949-X

CANADIAN ISBN: 0-523-43035-3

Cover illustration by Aleta Jenks

Printed in the United States of America

PINNACLE BOOKS, INC.
1430 Broadway
New York, New York 10018

9 8 7 6 5 4 3 2 1

JUDGEMENT AT POISONED WELL

1

Cord Diamondback felt the hangman's rope drop heavily around his neck like a fat lazy snake. But with his hands already tied behind his back, there wasn't anything he could do about it. Except wait. And scheme.

"Damn it, Bufford," the sheriff barked at his deputy. "Tighten that damn rope. *Tighter!*"

"It's pretty tight now, Sheriff," the young deputy protested.

"No it ain't. There's women and children present, Bufford. I want this sonofabitch's neck broke, not his feet dancing the Tennessee two-step for ten minutes while he chokes to death. This is a hanging, not a wedding. Use your damn head." He spit a brown stream of tobacco juice into the dirt and stomped away disgustedly to talk to a nearby group of onlookers.

The deputy shrugged, leaned over from atop his horse, and shoved the thick coiled knot tightly against Diamondback's neck until it pinched the skin. "Sorry," he muttered, loosening it a fraction.

Diamondback nodded thanks. Why not? No use

taking it out on the kid. Like everyone else in this mud-puddle town, the poor bastard was just doing what the sheriff told him. Besides, it was Cord's own stupidity and carelessness that had put him sitting under the business branch of a hanging tree.

All he had to do now was figure a way out. The deputy couldn't have been more than eighteen, with a nasty red rash under his neck from shaving too often. The tin star on his chest was still shiny and new, no scratches from hauling drunks to jail or rust from wading through cold rivers after rustlers. He wore it too high on his vest, Cord noticed, probably so he could always catch a proud glimpse of it out of the corner of his eye. His gun was an old Classic Peacemaker .44, seventeen dollars by mail order, worn too low on his hip, almost out of reach. He was just a skinny kid playing at being a lawman. But he was about to grow up fast . . . at Cord Diamondback's expense.

"Your first lynching, son?" Cord asked him quietly.

The boy looked confused by the question. "Ain't no lynchin' if the sheriff's doin' it."

"It is if there's no trial."

"Can't say. I don't know much about legal things, 'cept what Sheriff Tabor explains to me."

"Well, I *do* know," Diamondback said. "And there's got to be a trial. That's what the law books say. Otherwise it's murder."

The boy looked puzzled again and scratched his sore neck. "I don't know," he said, shaking his head. "Can't be illegal. This ain't the first time

Sheriff Tabor's done this. Ain't no one told him yet to stop. Not once."

The sheriff glanced over his shoulder, saw them talking and rushed over, muscling his thick bulldog body between the deputy's mustang and Diamondback's Appaloosa. "What's this scum saying to you, Bufford? What's he saying now?"

"Nothin', Sheriff. Honest."

Sheriff Tabor scowled up through his bushy black mustache at Diamondback. His teeth were stubby gray stones, his fat lips slightly discolored from tobacco. His eyes shone dimly like brass spittoons as he grinned. "Well, it don't matter what he says now, I s'ppose. The bastard'll be dead in a couple minutes. How's that grab ya, Diamondback?" He chuckled and went back to his cronies.

Cord Diamondback sat impassively in the saddle, the heavy rope cinched firmly against his throat. His back was straight and his demeanor was calm and confident. Something his late father, New Jersey's best trial lawyer, had taught him to do when facing a jury.

Compared to the rest of the tired, hollow men in the town, Diamondback stuck out like a wild stallion among a herd of plow horses. He was handsome and sure, with an almost cruel ruggedness to his features. *Satanic,* a girlfriend in college had once teased him after a night of inventive lovemaking in which he'd risked expulsion by smuggling her into his dorm room for the weekend. Indeed, his face was all sloping angles, sharp bones poking against pale skin. And it was that colorless skin that always seemed to attract women's attention. It gave his rugged features a certain aristocratic cast that suggested a volatile temper. He might be either gentle or rough. There was no way to predict. But while women studied the skin, it was the *eyes* that men noticed first. Dark dominating holes that seemed burned into his skull. Determining color was almost impossible, for they seemed to contain all colors at once, all crowded together with such density that no light escaped.

He stared out over the crowd of anxious townspeople. There weren't many, this being a town of less than four hundred, but those who were there seemed, if not enthusiastic, at least thankful for the diversion. Something exciting to break up another day like every other day in their hot dusty lives.

But Cord noticed one person out there who was different. Very different. She was tall for a woman, just shy of six feet. Her height and shapely figure were accented by her tailored outfit: expensive riding breeches, knee-high English riding boots, fancy riding gloves and a braided leather riding crop she tapped absently against her trim thigh. Though she stood in the middle of the crowd of milling townspeople, she stood alone. They had instinctively allowed for an invisible pocket around her, preventing any of the locals from brushing against her. It was a pocket created by money and social position, but enforced by the looming presence of a huge muscular man, not less than six feet four inches tall who stood directly behind her like a giant oak tree. He wore his Stetson low over his eyes, but the face was lean and hard as he scanned the crowd with obvious distaste, his right hand grazing the butt of his pistol.

The woman, on the other hand, looked only at Diamondback, a bemused grin playing on her thin straight lips, a distant twinkle in her arctic blue eyes. Her black hair shimmered in the sun like a slab of wet shale. Though she was in her early thirties, there was a thick lock of white hair at the base of her forehead, a kind of birthmark that cast a cold impersonal edge to her chiseled features. Still, her beauty glowed from the midst of the ragtag crowd, and her tall hard-nosed companion acted as if he knew he had something precious to protect.

Diamondback immediately dismissed her from his thoughts. He had no time to wonder about who was gathering to watch his execution or why. He had his own problems right now. Besides, he thought angrily, she looked too much like she was enjoying herself.

Diamondback squinted up into the bright afternoon sun. About three o'clock. Yeah, that'd be about right. He'd ridden into town early this morning after four long days on the trail. A hot meal, a hot bath and a nap on a real mattress. That's all he had in mind. The poker game had just been a way to relax.

Well, in a few minutes he was going to relax. Permanently.

He shifted slightly on his horse, feeling the pinch of rope circling his neck. Why poker, for God's sake? He didn't need the money. He had enough left from his last boxing match in Denver.

Enough to hold him over until he was needed for another judging job.

Why then had he sauntered over to that dirty table and asked to sit in for a few hands? He shrugged to himself. His horse, thinking the shrug was a signal to move, took a couple of steps forward, pulling the rope around Cord's neck even tighter. Quickly Cord clamped his knees against the Appaloosa's ribs and the horse backed up again. He took a deep breath, but the thin dry air scratched as it squeezed past the taut rope denting his throat.

Poker. He'd just wanted to unwind a bit before his bath. A friendly game with three old-timers and the one-legged bartender, who didn't have enough business to keep him leaning behind the bar. The game had been cordial, but quiet. No one was winning or losing much. No one cared. Cord had dropped about three dollars when Sheriff Tabor had swaggered into the saloon and joined in.

"Use another hand, boys?" he'd asked, sitting down before anyone could respond.

Cord had wanted to leave right then. But any abrupt movement to leave when a lawman enters the room tends to make people suspicious. Even in a tiny dirt town like this they'd have wanted posters on him under his real name, Christopher Deacon. Sure, he'd changed a few things since then—shaved his beard, let his hair grow—but eventually someone was bound to find something familiar about him. The crime was several years old, but they hadn't stopped looking for him, hadn't stopped calling him "the most wanted man in the West."

But Sheriff Tabor hadn't recognized him as Christopher Deacon. Nor had he seemed familiar with his growing reputation as Cord Diamondback, freelance judge and part-time prizefighter. He'd just nodded at the name noncommittally, the way a lot of people did while pondering whether or not Diamondback was an Indian name and whether they should treat him accordingly.

At first the cards had all fallen the sheriff's way, and he'd quickly amassed a large pile of money in front of him. He could do no wrong. He caught inside straights, flushes, full houses. Everything. He laughed loudly and told raunchy jokes, celebrating each winning hand with a quick shot of whiskey. But cards have a habit of running dry on you pretty damn suddenly, especially when drinking. Soon Sheriff Tabor began losing, and with each losing hand he continued to down a belt of whiskey. His mood went sullen and black, and he brooded angrily, insulting the players with each new hand.

Diamondback had waited for an opportunity to withdraw in a manner that wouldn't provoke the sheriff enough to jog his memory about wanted posters he may have seen. But just as Sheriff Tabor's luck went dry, Diamondback's began to flow. And soon an even larger pile of money was stacked in front of him. Leaving now while he was winning would only make matters worse. He'd decided to purposely lose the money to the sheriff over the next few hands.

But by then it was too late.

At the end of another losing hand, the sheriff jumped to his feet and drew out his Colt .44, leaning one hand on the table to steady himself as he wavered drunkenly. "You been cheatin' these folks for hours, Diamondback. I spotted your slick card handlin' right off, that's why I sat in. To get more evidence." No one else at the table said a word, either in protest or defense. They simply stared at the sheriff, who wiped his mouth with the back of his hand and continued. "Lucky for this town I know somethin about card slicks. And how to handle 'em."

That was twenty minutes ago.

Now Diamondback sat stiffly atop his horse and cursed himself for not pumping a few bullets through the sheriff's fat face. But he'd expected a stiff fine at worst. Not a lynching! A lot of these small towns were nothing more than traps, surviving off the money they "legally" robbed from strangers. And after collecting their phony fines, they usually let them go again. But not here. Not Sheriff Tabor.

"Okay, everybody here?" Sheriff Tabor mumbled around a hunk of tobacco he'd just bit off. He slipped the tobacco pouch back into his pocket and smiled at up Diamondback. In that same pocket was all the money he'd taken at gunpoint from Diamondback. "Let's see now, where's the best place to swat this pretty horse?" He traced an X with his finger on the horse's rump. At his touch, the Appaloosa took a nervous step forward. Sheriff Tabor laughed. "Whoa now, fella. Not too soon. You wouldn't want to rush the *judge* here, would ya?"

Surprised, Diamondback looked down at the sheriff.

"That's right, Diamondback." He sneered. "I heard of ya."

The deputy looked up from the knot he'd been checking where the rope was anchored around the tree trunk. "You say he's a judge, Sheriff?"

A frightened murmur ran through the crowd. Only the tall cool woman with the hulking companion was silent. She watched with a detached curiosity, as if it were all a stage play performed merely for her entertainment.

"Hell, not no real judge, Bufford. He ain't elected nor picked. Nothin' official. He's a whatdayacallit—a 'free-lance' judge. A fancy name for a gunfighter." He spit another muddy stream of tobacco juice against the hanging tree. "A boxer too. Seen him fight once in Carson City back when I was ridin' for the Garret spread. Damn near whupped that big feller to death. Lost me a week's pay on that one."

"Yeah, of course," the one-legged bartender said from the front of the crowd. He snapped his fingers in recollection. "Come to think of it, I did hear that name before. Diamondback. Read about you in the paper. You was up at Dog Trail, in Colorado. Took care of three gangs of outlaws."

"That's right," Cord said, realizing that this was no time for modesty. "And I settled that mining dispute over in Farrow County. With Marshall Condor." He listed a few more places and people, some of whom he'd been involved with, some he hadn't and some he just plain made up. It didn't matter. They all listened with rapt attention. And that's what he wanted.

He sensed a sudden shift in the crowd's attitude.

At first they'd been willing, if not to go along with their sheriff, at least to not interfere. Like a lot of these towns, he was both the town's law and the town's bully. And they were afraid enough of him to let him do whatever he wanted.

But now they weren't so sure. This time the victim was known, a minor celebrity, someone who'd been written about in the newspapers. Someone who knew famous lawmen. That confused them.

Sheriff Tabor sensed their shift in attitude too and hurried to complete the hanging. "It don't matter what he done before," he growled at the crowd. "He was cheatin' here. I seen him. Right, Peterson?"

The one-legged bartender shrugged. "None of us could really tell, Sheriff. We ain't seen many card slicks around here. 'Cept the ones you catch."

"Well, *I* can tell!" Sheriff Tabor shouted, his heavy face turning deep red, his thick jowls trembling with anger. "And I say he was cheatin', and I say we hang him now."

"I wasn't cheating," Cord said softly. "If I had been, I would have dropped you when you went for your gun."

"Ha!" The sheriff snorted. "You may be hot shit with a gun for an Injun, but around here ain't nobody faster than me. White, black, yellow *or* red." He turned to look at the crowd. "Ain't that right?"

There was some unenthusiastic muttering of agreement.

" 'Sides, I don't have to prove nothin to you. You ain't no judge here. Just a fella waitin to become a corpse." He took off his hat and raised it over the rump of Diamondback's horse. "The last thing you'll be judging is how long it takes you to die. *Heeya!*" he shouted and swatted Diamondback's horse on the backside. A puff of trail dust billowed up.

The horse whinied in protest, then bolted out at a full gallop.

Diamondback could feel the horse passing between his legs like the rush of a mighty river. The rope tightened around his neck with finality as his feet stretched toward the ground.

And found only air.

2

Dying wasn't half as bad as he'd feared.

He'd expected more pain, especially where the rope was supposed to snap his neck. But except for a tug against his windpipe, there was little pain.

Just a sensation of endless falling. Toward hell? he wondered. Is that how it happened? A dark steaming hole opened up in the ground and sucked you all the way down to a flaming inferno? He laughed dizzily at the thought. A strange last image for a man who believed in neither heaven nor hell.

Then his boot heels skidded across the dirt ground, dumping him on his backside. A sharp jolt of pain rattled his spine, slapping him out of his state of semiconsciousness. His eyes slowly focused on the sounds and movement around him.

"You damn idiot, Bufford!" Sheriff Tabor shouted. "What the hell you done that for?"

The young deputy climbed off his horse, slipping his heavy hunting knife back into the sheath on his belt. Diamondback shook his head to clear his vision. He noticed that the rope was cut where it had been fastened to the trunk of the tree.

"Well, I don't know for sure why I done it, Sheriff," the deputy shrugged. "I guess somethin' just didn't seem right here."

"Right! Didn't seem right! You moron, *I'll* tell you what's right. Now get him back up on his horse and fix that damn rope."

The kid scratched the rash under his neck and slowly shook his head. "I can't do that, Sheriff."

Sheriff Tabor looked stunned. Apparently no one had ever refused his command before, certainly not a kid so skinny his gunbelt kept slipping over his narrow hips.

"Now listen here, Bufford," the sheriff growled, his voice raspy with threat. "I ain't never killed a fella lawman before. But I gave you that star, and I can right enough take it away. Even if it's from your dead body." He pointed at Diamondback, who had risen to his feet, the severed noose dangling down his back. "Now you do what I say. Cinch that knot and put this Injun on his horse."

Bufford looked at the crowd, saw that no one there was going to back his play. He studied Sheriff Tabor again, watching the hand hovering near the gun, ready to draw. "Aw, hell." He shrugged defeatedly and walked over to lift Diamondback back onto a horse. The crowd sagged with resignation, their glimmer of hope stomped dead into the dust.

Cord caught a glimpse of the elegant statuesque woman and her companion, still observing the proceedings with amusement, but doing nothing to change the outcome.

The deputy tugged his own horse over, steadied him, and shuffled over behind Diamondback. Cord twisted around, fixing a cold dark stare on the boy. The deputy reddened with embarrassment and looked away. He reached for the rope, hesitated.

"Aw, hell," he said again, and spun suddenly around, pulling his old Peacemaker out of the worn leather holster. It was a slow and clumsy draw, but it caught Sheriff Tabor completely by surprise. He could only stand there and watch, his mouth hanging stupidly open, tobacco juice spilling down his chin. "Now, Sheriff," the deputy said, waving his gun nervously. "I don't want to use this on you, but I will if you make me. I'm just hopin' you won't make me."

The sheriff took a step toward Bufford. "Are you lookin' to die, boy?"

"Don't move, Sheriff. I'm already pretty spooked, and I'm liable to shoot anything that moves toward me. I mean that now."

"Think this through, boy. You don't want to die over some *stranger*, do ya?" He took another step forward.

"I don't want to die at all, if I can help it." Sweat dripped into his eye and he wiped his forehead with his sleeve. "But I don't want to be no murderer neither."

"I'm the sheriff, Bufford. How many times I tole ya, ain't no murder if I'm carryin out the law." Another step forward.

"Well, now I know what ya tole me. But this man here's been a judge, so I guess he knows somethin' about the law too."

"He ain't no real judge!"

"Well, as far as that goes, you ain't no real sheriff. I mean, we didn't elect you neither. When Sheriff Caufield died of fever, you just picked up the badge and told everyone you was sheriff."

"It's what you all wanted, isn't it?" Sheriff Tobor turned to the one-legged bartender. "Peterson?"

Peterson shifted on his crutch and shrugged.

The sheriff spun to the crowd in general. "I was the only one wanted the job. Right?"

The crowd stared back, looked at the ground but said nothing.

Sheriff Tabor's eyes blazed. "You mincing bunch of sheep! Who's been protecting you from the card slicks and conmen that been sweeping through our town lately? Me, that's who. And this is what I get for gratitude?"

"Hold on there, Tabor," Peterson said, hopping forward a step with his crutch. "We've all been paying you a monthly salary nearly twice what Sheriff Caufield got. And you been making plenty keeping the money you got from the men you hanged. So don't talk about gratitude. Ain't no one here grateful about you hanging all them strangers."

Sheriff Tabor fixed his stare on Bufford. He realized now that there was no point in arguing with the townspeople. Through the deputy's defiant act they'd all found a little courage. And talking wasn't going to change their minds. They needed to be reminded of why they feared him in the first place. They needed to see him in action.

"So, Bufford," he said softly, "what do you intend to do now? Let the card slick go?"

Bufford scratched his neck again and studied Diamondback. "Can't just let him go. Might be you was right about him. Have to think of somethin' else."

Murmured discussions of the problem rumbled through the crowd like distant thunder. Some had come for a hanging and didn't want to be disappointed. Others didn't want to anger Sheriff Tabor any more than he was already.

Diamondback turned toward the deputy. "I have an idea, Deputy."

The town's eyes focused on Cord's calm face. The dark eyes. The mouth like hammered copper, somewhere between a growl and a grin.

"We ain't int'rested in what you got to say," Sheriff Tabor snapped.

The deputy ignored his boss. "Go ahead, Mr. Diamondback. Looks like we could use your experience right now."

Cord nodded. "Well, the key question here is whether or not I cheated. Now—"

"Ain't no question!" Sheriff Tabor said. "It's fact!"

"Let him finish, Tabor," Peterson, the one-legged bartender, shouted. Mumbled agreement echoed from the crowd.

"Anyway," Cord continued, "I suggest that if I had been stupid enough to cheat while playing with a sheriff, I would have at least anticipated the possibility of him catching on. In which case I would have been ready to draw on him. Yet when Sheriff Tabor drew his gun, I did no such thing."

"He didn't, neither," Peterson agreed.

"Makes sense," someone in the crowd shouted.

Sheriff Tabor whirled toward the crowd. "That don't prove snake shit! The reason he didn't draw was 'cause I was too fast. Had my gun cocked and aimed 'fore he had time to fart." He turned back to Diamondback with a smug grin, his teeth swimming in tobacco juice and saliva. "Whatya say to that, Diamondass?"

Cord smiled. "There's one way to prove it."

"That's right, there is." Sheriff Tabor nodded at his depty. "Give the Injun his gun and let's get at it."

"I don't know," the kid said, scratching his neck again. "I don't want no more killing here that ain't necessary. Just ain't right."

Diamondback studied the deputy with new respect. He was brave and fair, a combination too rare out here. "Well, Deputy, we don't have to use loaded guns. We'll be able to see who is fastest that way as good as the other."

"That's a damn good idea, Mr. Diamondback. That oughta work just fine."

"The hell with that kid's stuff," the sheriff barked. "That sonofabitch called me a liar. I got the right to shoot it out with him for real. You owe me that much, Bufford."

The crowd muttered among themselves the merits of both sides before a strong clear voice silenced them.

"Excuse me, Deputy." The young woman with the white lock of hair was speaking. The crowd moved even farther away from her. "Might I offer a suggestion?"

"Kinda far from home, ain't ya, Mrs. Scarf?"

"Is that a polite way of telling me to mind my own business, Bufford?" She smiled.

The deputy reddened until his whole face matched his rash. "No, ma'am. Just that we don't see much of you around here."

"Nevertheless, I am entitled to my suggestions. You, of course, are free to ignore them."

Diamondback smiled. In just a few soft sentences, she'd managed to do what the sheriff with all his blustering and threats couldn't do. Control the deputy.

"I'm listenin', Mrs. Scarf," Bufford said politely.

She took a step forward, followed closely by her bodyguard. "Well, it seems to me that Mr. Diamondback's idea of using the empty guns, while certainly the more civilized approach, lacks a certain, um, practicality." She smiled, revealing a perfect set of glistening teeth. "Each man has made a claim. If the sheriff here is lying, then he deserves to die for putting this man's life in danger. However, if Mr. Diamondback here is lying, than the sheriff deserves an opportunity to vindicate himself and punish the man responsible."

Bufford pursed his lips in confusion. It sounded so reasonable. "But what about a trial and such?"

"Either way it goes, if you wait for a trial and a judge it could take months. Besides, I think it's gone too far for that now, don't you?"

"She's right, Bufford," the sheriff jumped in. "She's goodamn right. It's gone too far for that now. Me and him ought to do what's right, damn it."

Bufford turned to Diamondback. "What do you think, Mr. Diamondback?"

Diamondback remained expressionless. "You're in charge."

There was no point in saying anything else. The boy would have to make up his own mind and live with it. Cord didn't really care which way it went, though with loaded guns it would all be over with and he could be on his way. If he won.

He watched the kid agonize over what to do. The townspeople would offer no help either way. They didn't want any responsibility, which is how Tabor had so easily gained control of this crummy town. But when all the agonizing and worrying were done, Diamondback knew there was only one decision the deputy could make. If the sheriff was arrested, eventually he'd frighten someone into helping him escape and they'd be back where they started, only worse. If Diamondback was arrested, the sheriff would remain the sheriff, and because of their behavior, he'd be even more demanding. Their only chance now was for Diamondback to kill him.

"Okay," Bufford sighed resignedly. "Untie Mr. Diamondback and give him his gun. And clear out some space here."

"Won't take much space." The sheriff snickered as he backed up a couple steps, flexing his fingers. "I ain't seen a half-breed yet that could outdraw a white man."

One of the townsmen ran back from the sheriff's office with Cord's gun, a Smith & Wesson Shofield .45. Diamondback strapped it on with practiced precision, checking the cylinder to make sure it was loaded. He thumbed a cartridge into the hammer chamber which he usually left empty when riding. While tying the holster thong around his thigh, he glanced up and caught a glimpse of Mrs. Scarf, who had angled forward for a better view of the action. A cool smile rode her soft thin lips.

"All right now, make room!" Bufford yelled at the crowd, waving his arms. They shifted about like nervous cattle before a thunderstorm until Sheriff Tabor and Cord Diamondback stood face-to-face less than ten yards apart.

The deputy scratched his raw neck again and shrugged. "I guess I should count down or something so's you can . . ."

But Sheriff Tabor was already slapping at his gun, his thumb cocking the hammer as he slid it out of the holster, his finger tightening on the trigger as he thrust it toward Diamondback's stomach.

Too late.

The first bullet punched through Sheriff Tabor's chest, jerking him off his feet, and exploded through his back in a pink mist of blood. The second bullet ripped through his upper lip, shattering teeth and shredding skin before it burst out the back of his head, spraying the nearby crowd with splinters of skull and moist bits of sticky brain.

Sheriff Tabor flopped to the ground, his eyes still wide and confused, his right leg twitching crazily in some lurid death dance.

Diamondback kept his gun clutched in his hand. He wasn't sure how the crowd would react, and he wanted to be ready in case they had a sudden change of heart about the sheriff. Death sometimes had a way of ennobling the worst of men.

Apparently, the young deputy sheriff had the same fear, because he immediately began shooing the crowd away with broad waves of the hand. "Get goin, now. Go on back to work, folks. Come on, Mr. Peterson, you'd better see to your liquor stock 'fore someone sneaks in and guzzles it all up."

Peterson hobbled away on one leg and a wooden crutch, shaking his head at his friends. "Slickest piece of gunplay I ever seen." The townspeople muttered agreement as they accompanied him back to the saloon where they would spend the rest of the day exaggerating the details of the fight. Cord didn't mind. It was good for business.

The rest of the crowd broke up rather quickly. Cord tried to catch a glimpse of the stunning Mrs. Scarf, but she and her companion were already gone. Bufford was wiping the considerable sweat from his brow as he walked toward Diamondback.

"You can holster your gun now, Mr. Diamondback. Ain't gonna be no more gunplay."

Diamondback eased his gun back into its holster. The weight felt good on his hip, comfortable. He walked over to the bloody corpse of Sheriff Tabor and bent over the body. He brushed away a few fat flies that were already feasting at the mushy hole in the sheriff's face. Then he slipped his hand into the man's pocket.

"Whatchya doin?" the deputy called as he ran over, horrified.

"Getting my money back, Deputy." Diamondback plucked the wad of bills from the pocket and held them up. "This is mine."

Bufford scratched his rash thoughtfully.

Cord knew what was going through his mind now. He was staring at the money and calculating how easy it would be to pick up where the sheriff left off. Maybe not hanging people, but still invoking phony laws with which to levy huge fines. Most folks would sooner pay than fight. Cord watched the deputy's eyes flicker over the money as he licked his lips thirstily. Easy money. If he took it, or any part of it, he'd be starting down the same road as Sheriff Tabor. If he didn't, well, he had a chance. And so did the town.

"Something wrong, Deputy?" Cord asked.

"Huh?" The deputy dragged his eyes away from the money. "Nope, Mr. Diamondback, nothin's wrong. You can go anytime now."

Diamondback clapped him on the shoulder and smiled. "It doesn't get any easier, son. Ever."

"What doesn't?"

"Temptation."

Bufford flushed and lowered his eyes. "I don't s'ppose you'll be stayin' here in town much longer, Mr. Diamondback?"

"Is that a request, Deputy?"

"No, sir, just a question. Maybe even a suggestion. Sheriff Tabor wasn't without a few friends of the same kind as him. I'd hate to see more trouble here."

Diamondback nodded. "I'm just staying long enough to get what I'd originally come for. A hot bath and a hot meal. I'll skip the nap on the soft mattress."

"Well, you can get both them things at the Timberline Hotel across the street there. Just be careful."

"Thanks. A couple questions first, if you don't mind."

"Won't know if I mind till you ask."

Cord smiled. "Fair enough. First, who is Mrs. Scarf?"

The deputy hitched his drooping gunbelt and sighed. "Hell of a woman, ain't she? Widowed a couple years back and now she owns the biggest damn spread in the state over by Poisoned Well. Damn handsome woman, I'd say." He gazed off for a moment, lost in some fantasy, before grinning sheepishly. "What was the other question?"

"I'm curious. Considering your differences, why did Sheriff Tabor make you his depty in the first place?"

"Had to, I s'ppose." He shrugged. "He was my uncle."

"Mr. Diamondback?" The hand clamped on his shoulder like a heavy saddle. The voice was brusk and challenging, used to getting its way.

Cord was standing in the drab lobby of the Timberline Hotel. He brushed the hand off his shoulder as he turned to face the man who'd stopped him. He recognized the towering companion of Mrs. Scarf, whose right hand still hovered near his gun butt.

"Mrs. Scarf wants to see you."

"Thanks for the message." Diamondback turned and started back toward the hotel desk. The meaty hand dropped on his shoulder again. Heavier.

"I said Mrs. Scarf wants to see you. Now."

"I don't want to see Mrs. Scarf."

The tall man smiled a thin mean smile and tilted his Stetson back from his narrow eyes. "Then I guess you and me got trouble," he said and threw his huge fist at Cord's face.

3

The fist came hurtling at him like a flaming meteor. Behind it was all the power the man's 235-pound body could pack, enough to crush whatever it hit.

But Diamondback wasn't going to give him the chance. Instinctively, he bobbed under the looping swing, letting it brush over his left shoulder. Then he twisted his body upward, digging his fist into the man's stomach like a pickax.

"*Oooof,*" the big man gasped, folding in half and grabbing for his stomach. Desperately he tried to suck air into his empty lungs.

Cord looked at the helpless coughing man a moment, debating whether or not to hit him again just for the inconvenience he'd caused. But he just sighed and walked away. He'd had enough excitement for one day.

"Diamond . . . back!" the big man snarled in a combination of hate and pain as he forced himself to straighten up. Once upright, he faced Cord and squared off. His right hand flew to his holstered gun.

Cord covered the few feet between them in one

giant leap, double pumping his left jab into the man's eye, then smashing his cheek with a right cross.

The gunman's head snapped back and forth like a flag in a high wind before his eyes rolled up and he sagged to the floor face-first.

Diamondback stepped over the unconscious body and walked to the front desk where the hotel clerk had been watching the proceedings with bored annoyance.

"I'd like a hot bath and a hot meal."

"Sure you do, son," the clerk said. He was a grizzled old man with a dirty gray beard and no teeth. "And I'd like to be young again. We all gotta live with disappointment."

Cord smiled. "This is a hotel, isn't it?"

"Hell, no! It's a goddamn gymnasium. Didn't you catch the sparring match on the way in?"

"I'm sorry about that, but he started it."

"Ohhhh, he started it. Well, now, that's different, ain't it. I guess that means my lobby ain't been disturbed. Nor my hotel's reputation hurt. Nor my—"

"How much to restore your hotel's, uh, dignity?"

The old man tugged on the wispy end of his ragged beard. His pale blue eyes narrowed slyly. "Well, now, there's two bits for creating a disturbance in my lobby."

Cord tossed a quarter on the desk.

"And then there's two bits for chasin' away potential customers."

Cord dropped another quarter on the desk.

"And, uh, two bits for me to lug him outta the

middle of the room. He ain't no lightweight, ya know."

Cord threw a dollar on the desk and scooped up the two quarters. "There's an extra two bits for you to tell me your dinner menu."

The old man swept the dollar into his pocket without thanks. "We got steak and eggs in the dining room."

"What else?"

The old man snorted. "Nothin' else. Steaks and eggs is what we got, and if you want a hot meal it's what you'll eat."

Cord laughed. "You make it hard to refuse your hospitality."

"Don't sass me, boy," the old man warned, shaking a bony finger. "I can still handle myself in a fight."

"Sorry, mister," Cord said. "Didn't mean any disrespect."

The hotel clerk seemed somewhat mollified by that. "Better take your bath first, though. I got a Chinaman that fills the tubs and he only works another half hour."

"Fine."

A low groan rumbled from across the lobby as Mrs. Scarf's companion began to slowly stir.

Cord hooked a thumb over his shoulder at the man as he spoke to the clerk. "And see that he finds his way back to Mrs. Scarf."

"Sure thing," the old man nodded and stuck out his open palm. "But that'll be another two bits for delivering a parcel."

Diamondback climbed naked into the steaming

tub, slowly easing himself deeper until the hot water lapped against his thick muscular chest. His entire body was ridged with hard sculpted muscles, which in the water looked like polished stones at the bottom of a mountain stream. With a contented sigh, Cord rested his head on the back of the tub and closed his eyes. He sank a little deeper, allowing the soothing water to swirl around his sore neck where the hanging rope had rubbed the skin raw.

Washing could come later. For the next hour he intended to just soak. Soak and sigh. Doze if he wanted. Let his toes and fingers pucker, he didn't care. The door was locked, the water was hot and for once all was right with the world.

He could feel the wet heat gently relaxing every part of his body. Every part but one. The part that needed it most.

His damned back. Grotesque. Freakish.

The scars rode his back like separate living creatures, fat leeches forever feeding. Too thick in some places for him to feel anything, either pain or pleasure. Or was that just his imagination? His way of dealing with the hideous reminder that would never go away as long as he lived. They laid across his back in the bizarre crisscrossed pattern that had prompted the Shoshone Indians to name him after the diamondback rattlesnake. They had meant it as an honor and he had adopted it as his new name. Hell, any name was better than his real one now.

Christopher Deacon, he said bitterly to himself. He didn't dare say it aloud, not even alone.

There wasn't a lawman or bounty hunter in the

West who wasn't familiar with the name. Or a citizen, for that matter, who wouldn't like to collect the biggest reward ever offered. Even the youngest schoolchildren would recognize the jagged white scars furrowed across his back. And for that reason he allowed people to think he was part Indian, though his pale skin always confused them. And he made sure never to expose his naked back to anyone, even in the most intimate situations. Those scars were the permanent brand that kept him running all these years. Would keep him running the rest of his life. He thought back to that evening again, the night of his bloody revenge. The night that had started his endless wandering. He smiled grimly, knowing he would do it all again. Almost wishing he could.

He took a deep breath, enjoyed the warm steam filling his lungs. Steak and eggs. After four days of beef jerky and beans, that would be—

A faint scraping noise outside the door.

He opened his eyes and quietly reached for his gunbelt which was draped over a nearby chair. His hand was only halfway there when the door was kicked open and a Colt Frontier double-action .45 was shoved into his face.

The .45 was gripped in the meaty hand of Mrs. Scarf's companion, who stood directly behind her, sneering at Diamondback through bared teeth and a swollen left eye. A purple-and-yellow bump as big and shiny as a brass doorknob rode his right cheek. His finger twitched anxiously on the trigger.

"No need to *rise*," Mrs. Scarf smiled, her eyes sliding appreciatively down Cord's body.

Cord eased back into the tub, both to mollify the gunman and to hide his exposed back.

Mrs. Scarf allowed her eyes to linger on Cord's nakedness before returning to his eyes. "Mr. Grodin here delivered your message, Mr. Diamondback. I decided to drop by and make an appointment."

"Fine. How about a week from Wednesday? Around noon?"

"Listen, funny man," Grodin growled, stepping forward. "I owe you. Don't make me collect right now."

Mrs. Scarf laid a light restraining hand on Grodin's arm and he immediately backed off. "I think I can handle things from here, Jim. Just give me your gun and wait for me in the lobby."

"But, Mrs. Scarf—"

She smiled coldly, revealing only the edge of the ice beneath. Grodin crumpled faster than he had from Diamondback's punches. He handed her his gun and started out of the room.

"Close the door, please, Jim."

Grodin turned, shot a white-hot glare at Cord, then closed the door. They could hear his heavy footsteps stomping down the hall.

She kept the gun pointed at Cord's chest as she spoke. "Well, I must say, you certainly have a boxer's body. Hard all over." She grinned wickedly. "Except for one place. What's the matter, Mr. Diamondback, have a debilitating accident? Kicked by a horse, perhaps?"

"No, ma'am. I just have to see something that interests me first."

A dark crimson flush burned across her cheeks like a brushfire as the smile thawed from her lips.

There was an angry edge to her voice when she spoke again, like a saw cutting through hard pine. "Do you know who I am, Diamondback?"

"A rude woman?"

"A rude *rich* woman. One who owns a lot of land, cattle and men."

"Good, because you owe me fifty cents. That's what this bath cost me."

She smiled again, pulled around the chair with Cord's gunbelt and sat down only a foot away from the tub. Her gun remained leveled at Cord's chest. "Are you an Indian, Mr. Diamondback?"

"No."

"Then why didn't you deny it earlier when the sheriff kept calling you one?"

"Why should I? It's not something to be ashamed of."

"Well, well, a free thinker in the Wild West." She brushed the white lock of hair off her forehead. "My foreman tells me you have quite a reputation as a private judge. Sorry to say I'd never heard of you before."

Cord reached for the ball of rough homemade soap. Mrs. Scarf thrust the gun out. "Look, this water's starting to cool down. I'd like to soap off while it's still warm. You mind?"

She shook her head. "You look like you need a good washing."

Cord lathered the soap on his face, scrubbed the skin with his fingers, then dipped his head forward in the water to rinse off.

"Just a few more questions, Mr. Diamondback, then . . ."

Cord lifted his head out of the water, turned to

face Mrs. Scarf and spit a mouthful of warm soapy water in her eyes. She jumped back with a surprised squeal, and Cord lashed out, wrapping his steel fingers around her thin wrist. With a strong jerk, he pulled her out of the chair and over the edge of the tub into the water. Soapy waves slapped the sides of the tub, splashing over the edges and onto the wooden floor.

While holding her head under the water, Cord quickly twisted the gun out of her hand and tossed it skidding across the floor. Only then did he release his grip on the back of her neck.

She snapped her head out of the water with a loud choking cough. Water dribbled out of her mouth as she gulped for air.

"I . . . kill . . . you," she sputtered. Her wet hair curled crazily around her face like soggy seaweed. She grasped the sides of the tub and tried to get up, but Cord pulled her back down, splashing more water onto the floor.

The broken door was suddenly flung open and the old hotel clerk marched in carrying a plate with a burned steak and runny eggs. "What the hell's goin on here, mister? I was bringin' you your dinner and . . . Holy pig shit, lookit this mess!"

"Nothing to worry about," Diamondback winked. "Just having a little fun."

Mrs. Scarf tried to sputter a protest, but Cord shoved her back under the water.

"I'm teaching her to swim."

The old man shook his head with disgust. "Sure didn't figure Mrs. Scarf for this—seems kinda strange. Rich folks, though, ya never know." He set the plate on the chair while he surveyed the room. "Still, it's gonna cost ya, son. Two bits to mop up the floor. A dollar to fix the door. Fifty cents for another person bathing. Then there's your hot dinner. Let's see, that's—"

"Put it on my bill. I'll pay later."

"You bet your ass you will, son," he muttered as he walked out, slamming the door closed behind him.

Cord released the thrashing Mrs. Scarf and watched her repeat her previous coughing and gasping. "You fucking sonofabitch bastard. You goddamn—"

He put his hand firmly on the top of her head. "You want more?"

"No," she said quickly. "Enough."

"Fine. Now we can talk. Only this time I'll ask the questions."

She slumped back against the tub, her knees bent and legs spread. Cord's knees were bent too, but pressed together in a protective position. "Ask." She sighed.

"First, why did you force the gunfight out there with Sheriff Tabor?"

"I didn't force anything."

Cord frowned, reached for her head.

"Okay, okay. I *encouraged* it."

"Why?"

"I wanted to see how good you were with a gun."

"Why?"

"I'm looking to hire capable men right now. You looked like a good prospect."

"What if I had lost?"

She smiled. "Then I would have hired Sheriff Tabor."

"I see. Well, that's straight enough."

"Anyway, you won, so I'm offering you the job." She shifted uncomfortably. "Mind if I take these boots off? They're like lead when they get wet." She didn't wait for an answer, but tugged them off and threw them over the side of the tub. Then she peeled off her leather gloves and tossed them over her shoulder.

"What do you need 'capable' men for?" Cord asked.

"Protection. I own a lot of cattle and cattle need to graze. They've always grazed in the valley over by Poisoned Well. But recently some of the little ranchers have banded together and started fencing off the valley with barbed wire. Well, my husband didn't allow any barbed wire in the valley and I won't either."

"Whose land is it. Legally."

"Theirs, legally," she said, her eyes glaring like a branding iron. "But it's traditionally been open range for the last fifty years. And most of those pissant ranchers just moved in within the last few years. They're not only fencing it off, but they're bringing in sheep which will ruin the grass for cattle. Without that grazing, half of my herd will likely starve."

"And you want me to arbitrate. As a judge."

She laughed scornfully, like the clinking of icicles. "No, Mr. Diamondback. In this matter I'm the only judge. I want you as a hired gun. Nothing more."

"I'm a judge, not a gunman, Mrs. Scarf."

"Suit yourself. But what I need is a gunman, someone smart enough to know the difference between killing and getting killed. I pay damn well to men who have that knowledge, and can enforce it. If you change your mind, it's only another three days to Poisoned Well. Anyone there can direct you to my ranch." She leaned forward, one hand on the side of the tub, the other groping for balance under the water. Her hand brushed Cord's penis, now clearly erect. She glanced up into his dark eyes and stony face, a sly grin on her thin lips. "It appears that you've seen something that interests you after all, Mr. Diamondback."

Cord said nothing. Made no move. This wasn't the kind of woman to get involved with. Not now. There was too much ice in her blood, granite in her heart. After all, she had been willing to risk his life in a shoot-out just to see how fast he was. Merely on the chance that she might be able to use him. She was powerful, and that power had made her arrogant. But it also enhanced her beauty, like the pure blue in the hottest part of a flame.

She started to rise, water pouring out of her clothes at every opening. But as she got halfway to her feet, she pretended to slip and tumbled forward toward Diamondback. His powerful arms reached up and caught her around the waist in mid-fall, held her suspended and breathless for a moment, then slowly lowered her down until she was draped across his naked body. Her face was less than an inch from his, but still he made no move.

She did.

Her mouth was open as it lunged against his,

lips struggling against each other, firm tongues probing like wet fingers. Her eyes remained open, staring into his as she wriggled against his nakedness, one hand hooked behind his neck, the other brushing across his massive chest, occasionally pressing fingertips into a hard muscle. His solid body delighted her, seeming so much as if carved from some exotic tropical wood. But not like a statue. He was too human for that. No, she could feel the throbbing of his blood surging through the enormous veins that mapped his body.

Her clothes came off in a frenzy of movement; blouse, pants, underwear, all tossed over the side of the tub, landing with a soggy splat. It didn't matter. Everything outside that tub was another world, a dim foreign world as distant as Asia or Africa. All she or Cord could think about was what was going on right now, right there in the sloshing warm water.

When the last piece of clothing was gone, they faced each other, both on their knees. Her wet skin glistened. Her body was slender yet firm, the result of working her ranch, not just overseeing it.

Cord let his rough fingers glide gently over the smooth skin of her shoulders, tracing the curves of her breasts with such gentleness that she shuddered with desire. Her nipples budded out hungrily, dark and enticing.

He lowered his head and took one in his mouth, nipping the end playfully with his teeth. She gasped and pulled his head tighter against her breast. "Suck it," she cried. "Suck it all."

Cord obliged, taking almost her entire breast

into his mouth. He felt her hard nipple tickle the back of his throat.

She pressed closer to him, panting shallowly, hugging his head firmly with one hand, groping in the water for his penis with the other. When she found it, she wrapped her cool fingers around the tip and squeezed.

Aggressive women didn't bother Cord. In fact, he respected a woman for getting what she wanted. But in all his experience, he'd never encountered a woman as passionately determined to get what she wanted as Mrs. Scarf.

Suddenly she had her tongue back in his mouth, licking and wrestling his tongue with urgency. Then she pushed his shoulders until he was leaning against the back of the tub. She scooped her hands under his hips, lifting them out of the water. With each hand gripped tightly on a buttock, she leaned her head forward, flicking her tongue at his penis. Gently biting the end. Finally swallowing the entire shaft until her chin brushed his balls.

He watched her head bobbing in front of him, her cheeks slapping water with each downward thrust. Occasionally he felt her teeth scraping the length of his penis, sending a spasm of painful pleasure through his stomach. With expert concentration, she brought him to the edge several times, his heart thumping, penis red and stretching. Each time she would stop, lick a thick drop of milky liquid from the tip, then swallow it again, all the time staring into his eyes, her lips smiling mischievously around his throbbing penis.

Finally she stopped, leaned back against the tub and lifted her legs out of the water, hooking each ankle over the side of the tub. She reached back into the water, found his penis, and pulled it toward her open vagina. Cord did not resist. She guided it to the fleshy opening, slippery even underwater, and urged it deep into her body.

Cord took a deep breath. The smell of the homemade soap stung his nose. Then he smelled the other scent, her musky, feral odor, intensified by the warm water like a pile of autumn leaves after a rain.

So far he had allowed himself to be led by her desires. But now it was his turn. Now he would take over. He slipped his muscular arms around her back, with one hand clutching both her firm buttocks. Then he thrust forward, his hips bumping soundlessly against hers. At first he rocked softly in the water, creating a soothing rhythm as water slapped the sides of the tub. He felt her fingernails raking his neck. When they started to drift toward his back, he shifted his shoulders and brought them back up to his neck. Even now he was aware that his scars had to remain hidden.

Now he increased his pace, thrusting into her again and again as water churned and foamed around them like an ocean storm. She grabbed on to his neck as if she feared he could buck her out of the tub. She moaned softly at first, matching his rhythm. But as his thrust became more insistent and powerful, her moans became louder.

"Come on," she urged hoarsely, her eyes clenched. "Come *on*!"

They moved faster now, her nails imbedded in his flesh, his penis embedded in hers. Each thrust seemed to send him deeper into her body, and deeper yet. Something that was more a part of her body now than his. She reached down with one hand and cupped his balls tightly, squeezing with each thrust.

"Now," she panted. "Come . . . now. Now!"

She gave one final squeeze and Cord's back suddenly arched, muscles straining across his shoulders. He came with a dizzying urgency that seemed to last for several minutes. He felt the muscles of her vagina rippling along his penis, tiny fingers milking out every last drop. Her body began to move faster and faster. Her breathing was only short sobs now as she pumped against him, harder and faster. She was slamming against him now with such force he thought she might hurt herself. Then her eyes widened, her mouth opened to reveal sharp clenched teeth and a long low moan echoed through the room. She strained against him, her ankles digging into his buttocks, her hips vibrating.

"Christ! Jesus!" She gasped, shivering once, then again. A long windy sigh blew out of her mouth as she slumped back against the tub. "Damn, that's good," she said.

Cord eased himself out of her and leaned back against the other end of the tub.

She smiled, her foot stroking his shoulder. "I was right about you."

"How so?"

"I said I was looking for capable men. You're certainly more than capable." She brushed the white lock of hair from her forehead. "So how about it?"

Cord looked puzzled. "How about what?"

"The job. How about the job? Good pay." She raised a suggestive eyebrow. "Certain privileges."

"You want a judge?" he asked flatly.

"I told you, I'm the only goddamn judge in that valley. Maybe with some poor slobs you're something else. But with me you're a gun, nothing more."

Cord stood up, water cascading down his hard body. He stepped out of the tub and quickly dressed. Then he walked over to the soggy pile of clothes she'd stripped off earlier. He snatched up her pants, reached into the pocket, pulled something out, then tossed the pants into the tub. Water splashed into her face.

"What the hell do you think you're doing?" she yelled.

He held up the fifty-cent coin he'd taken from her pocket. "For the bath." He smiled and walked out the door.

4

The shrill scream ripped through the still Nevada air like a jagged claw of lightning.

"What in hell—?" Cord mumbled, suddenly startled from his reading. He looked up from his book, leaned forward in the saddle and glanced around the peaceful valley. His first thought was that whatever caused that horrifying sound couldn't possibly be human. But then again he'd never heard any kind of animal howl with such wretched fear and pain.

A cold shiver crawled across his neck.

Instinctively he jerked back on the Appaloosa's reins, but the big horse shook its head briskly and snorted in protest. Frightened by the scream and confused by Diamondback's command to stop rather than run away, the horse reared back on its hind legs and skittered sideways, uprooting heavy clumps of fresh grass. Cord's thick leather-bound book flapped out of his hands as he yanked firmly on the reins, wrestling the terrified horse to a halt.

He hesitated a minute, listening. His own heart

thumped steadily while his horse nervously tattooed the ground with his right hoof.

"What in hell?" he repeated and licked his lips. But there was no moisture. His tongue scraped roughly along his parched lips like a desert lizard bellying across a dusty rock.

Gently stroking his horse's neck with one hand, Cord let his other hand drift toward his pistol. He stood up in the stirrups for a better look, twisting around in the saddle as his dark eyes explored every grassy knoll. But there was nothing. No sinister outlaws. No glint of sunlight reflecting off a hidden rifle. Just acres and acres of sun-washed valley. Breezy open ranges so lush and beautiful that Cord felt a familiar ache to change his name for the last and final time and settle down. For good. He laughed harshly and shoved that dangerous thought out of his mind. He knew too well the reasons he never could. Nothing had changed.

He cupped his hand behind one ear, swiveled his head like a weather vane. Nothing. The only sound was the easy wind skimming across the waves of long sweet-smelling grass.

Damn peculiar.

He relaxed back into his saddle and shook his head. How could any sound so tortured come from a serene place like this? He must have imagined it. After all, forty-eight hours ago he'd escaped from a hanging, gunned down a sheriff, made wet and sudsy love to one of the most powerful women in the state—certainly one of the most passionate—and had been riding under a hot Nevada sun for the past six hours. Besides, he'd

Judgement at Poisoned Well

been following his usual habit on long rides of reading. Diamondback devoured books with the same appetite some men showed for whiskey or steaks. It didn't matter what kind of book—philosophy, history, science, novels—he read whatever he could scare up. This time he'd been reading a curious new novel written by General Lewis Wallace, the territorial governor of New Mexico. The same man who'd defended Washington against the Confederates during the Civil War. It was a strange book for a soldier to write, all about Romans and Christianity. *Ben-Hur*. He smiled. Certainly there was enough torment and despair in those pages to inspire an imagined scream.

On the other hand . . .

Maybe this valley wasn't as peaceful as it seemed. Not if one were to believe the fiery Mrs. Scarf. Not to someone who's hiring gunmen as anxiously as she was. And just down the road ten miles was the town of Poisoned Well. The eye of the hurricane.

Poisoned Well. An uninviting name, Cord thought. Perhaps he'd made a mistake in coming here. He didn't have a job. And he wasn't welcome by either side; certainly Mrs. Scarf had made that clear. But Cord Diamondback was nothing if not enterprising. If there was a fight boiling down here, there was opportunity for a man like him. Not just as a mindless hired gun. That kind of job was short on money and long on danger.

No, he was a judge, educated in the law and experienced in the ways of enforcing it. A man who believed fiercely in justice. Fiercely enough to have committed a "crime" that would never be forgotten—although it had been committed in the name of justice. Cord knew that sometimes justice went beyond the law. And when it did, Cord Diamondback was the one people hired. He had lost every person he'd ever loved, and his work was all he had left. So he cherished and defended it as one would a family. It was what he did best. He'd been away from it too long now, more than three months, filling in time picking up prizefights. But maybe, if the trouble was bad enough here—and the stakes were high enough—he could promote himself into just such a job. Despite what Mrs. Scarf had said.

"To hell with imagined screams." He sighed, climbing down from the saddle to retrieve his book. "I'm probably just not used to anything as peaceful as this place."

But suddenly there it was again!

The piercing scream scraped across his spine and sent an icy wave of adrenaline splashing through his tensed stomach. This time it was even louder, echoing through the valley like a ghostly demon. And this time it was even more tormented than before, though now he was certain it was human. Just barely.

He swung back onto his Appaloosa, kicking his heels into its ribs. The horse bolted off in the direction of the scream, somewhere over the north ridge of the valley. Even as he gripped the reins and gigged his horse, Cord wondered why he was doing this. It's none of my business, he told himself. I have enough trouble of my own, enough people on my trail to butt my battered nose into someone else's troubles. Especially for free.

But even as these thoughts sifted through his mind he quickened his horse's pace. He knew there were some urges beyond reason. And there was something so basic, so elemental in that terrified cry that no human could resist answering it. It was the desperate plea of someone caught in a nightmare from which they couldn't awaken. And as such, he knew it touched on a rich deep horror every person shares.

Diamondback whacked the horse's flank with his hat and leaned forward into the saddle, letting the warm Nevada wind dry the sweat from his face. Sweat that just a few minutes ago hadn't been there.

When the scream came again it was weaker, little more than a choked gasp, the throat scraped raw from its previous efforts. Cord felt a sympathetic twinge in his own throat where the hangman's rope had chafed his skin.

"Damn!" he cursed, urging his horse up the knoll with his heels. When he reached the top he would have a wide view of the valley on the other side.

And hopefully of the screaming man.

The galloping Appaloosa's thick muscles rolled under Diamondback's taut body like powerful ocean waves as they plunged up the steep hill. The animal's long damp neck was bent low for balance and his hooves pounded out clods of grass as he struggled upward.

Thirty feet to go.

Twenty feet.

Diamondback prodded again with his heels.

Ten.

Five.

And over the top.

Diamondback reined in the horse with a firm tug as he surveyed the scene below. His dark eyes flashed horror and disbelief.

"My God!" he gasped.

5

"For God'd sake!" the man sobbed weakly. "Help me. *Help me!*"

Diamondback didn't hesitate. He drove his horse over the edge and down the hill at full gallop, his teeth clenched in grim rage as he charged ahead. A sudden gust of wind lifted his hat off his head and swirled it away. His long brown hair whipped across his ears and neck, his dark eyes squinting against the harsh wind. His neck muscles bulged like thick braided ropes as he yelled for his horse to go faster. His nose pressed against its sweating earthy coat. He rode now with the same fierce intensity as he had as a cavalry soldier against No Warning and the Kiowas during the Red River War.

Even so, he feared he would be too late.

The man was less than a quarter of a mile away now, but even his slightest whimper of pain was amplified by the breeze. Cord tried to go faster, but the Appaloosa was already thundering across the ground at top speed. He clutched the reins tighter, not believing the sight even as he dashed toward it. Too cruel. Too inhuman.

The helpless man was bound to a gnarled tree, not with rope, but with something much stronger. And more effective.

Barbed wire.

Whoever had done this had been thorough. Not only had they wrapped it dozens of times around his chest and legs, pinning his arms helplessly to his sides, but they'd also strung it tautly around his neck and forehead. Even from here, Cord could see the twisted metal barbs gouging the man's neck and face like tiny devil's horns. Deep furrows of flesh had been raked out of his throat as he'd struggled to scream for help. Thick drops of blood dripped down his neck and forehead, blossomed from his bound wrists, welled from his chest where the metal thorns had ripped his shirt and skin as easily as newspaper.

But that wasn't what caused the desperate screams. A man could wait patiently out here in that condition with reasonable assurance that a rider or cowhand would discover and help him. Painful, sure. But not fatal.

Yet his tormentors had not been content merely to bind him to the tree with barbed wire. They had gone one horrible step further.

Next to the tree was an old wooden buckboard loaded high with bales of new No. 9 barbed wire, factory-painted red. Just like the wire wrapped around the man. But with a deadly difference.

The buckboard was also filled with fire.

Bright ragged flames leaped from the charred buckboard, two wheels of which had already collapsed, spilling flaming spears of wood across the ground. Because the wagon was so close to the tree, some of the flames had hungrily jumped the short distance to the lush overhanging branches, and the tree burned now with a roaring fury. A rushing river of gray smoke poured upward into the sky like an upside-down waterfall. Red and yellow flames cackled like witches as they consumed the tree.

Fortunately for the bound man, the fire had started at the top and had to slowly gnaw its way down.

Unfortunately, it was now only inches away from his head.

"Please, *please*" the man pleaded to Diamondback as the flames licked the trunk next to his face. "Oh, God, please."

Cord closed the distance within seconds, leaping off the Appaloosa before it had come to a complete halt. He fell to his knees, scrambled to his feet and ran toward the tree and the writhing man.

"Thank God," the man wept. "Thank God!"

The flames had chewed up most of the bark and was now nipping at the man's head. He dragged his head away, ripping skin from his throat and forehead. Yet the fire dripped down the tree even further. One flame singed his ear.

Cord reached out and grabbed a handful of wire at the man's chest. But the fire had heated the metal, branding a sizzling line along the inside of Cord's palm. He could smell the bitter scent of his own burnt flesh. Still, he didn't let go, continuing to tug the wire, trying to loosen it. No good. Too tight. He traced the joint where it had been tied, but was unable to budge it.

"Hurry," the man gasped. *"Please, God, hurry."*

Cord glanced into the man's desperate face, saw he was just barely out of his teens, his face smooth and boyish. A gray film of soot covered his skin, streaked with tears. His swollen eyes begged Cord for help.

The fire was spreading even faster now, nibbling at the man's leg. His pants suddenly caught fire and he jerked his leg, driving the barbs deeper into his flesh. He howled with pain.

Without hesitation or concern about his secret scars, Diamondback tore off his own shirt and swatted the flames out. But by then the man's shirt began to smoke. There wasn't much time left. The flames were already surrounding the young man.

Cord pulled out his gun and fired point-blank into the wire six inches to the right of the boy's head. The bullet severed the wire with a twang and buried itself into the tree with a splash of splinters. Cord fired again. And again. Each time he severed another wire. The man could move his head and neck now, but his voice was gone. He could no longer speak, merely grunt his pleas. Cord kept firing. The smell of gunsmoke, mixed with the fire's smoke, hung heavy in the air. But there were too many wires; they'd wrapped him in a cocoon of barbed wire. Thirty or forty strands still wound around him. Still, Cord fired shot after shot, reloading and firing again.

The wires loosened and Cord reached in, pulling the severed strands free, burning his hand on the hot metal, cutting his fingers on the sharp barbs. The young man could move more now, but he was still strapped to the tree by a dozen more wires. Cord reloaded, already knowing it was too late.

Too late by a minute. Too late by a lifetime.

The fire had dominated the buckboard and the tree. And finally it dominated the young man. Cord continued to fire into the wire, even when he could see that it was hopeless. Flames like burning fingers reached around the trunk to clutch at its victim. The first finger touched the top of his head, and Cord backed away as the young man's hair whooshed in a sudden crown of fire. The man choked out a rasping scream, but even that was cut off as the fire ignited his face. Cord watched as the smooth skin bubbled up into boiling blisters, then peeled away in blackened layers of crispy skin like dried leaves.

And then everything was flame.

Diamondback staggered backward, his hands shading his face from the intense heat. Swallowing thickly, he swung his gun around and fire three more bullets. Into the young man's chest. The body flexed, then sagged with relief against the barbed wire. Diamondback's eyes were fixed morosely on the man as the rest of his body was engulfed by waves of flame. He watched the body shrivel and blacken, saw a gnarled black hunk drop from the body like a slab of bark. It was a hand.

He had to walk a quarter of a mile to fetch his Appaloosa, but he didn't mind. He needed the time to breathe, to force himself to swallow the sour bile in his mouth. And to think.

It was possible that whoever had done this hadn't

meant for the tree to catch fire, had only meant to scare him. But that didn't matter to the boy, just barely a man. He was dead.

The range war here over barbed wire was more vicious than even Mrs. Scarf had indicated. And for whoever had set this fire, it promised to get much worse. If Diamondback had his way.

6

"That a dead body, mister?"

Cord glanced down at the little girl in the blue sunbonnet and matching dress. He said nothing.

"You a bounty hunter, mister?"

Cord kept riding, pulling the second horse behind him. It was one of the buckboard horses that had been freed prior to the fire. The killers had more respect for horseflesh than human flesh. Tied to the horse's back were the charred remains, barely recognizable as human. They were wrapped in Cord's yellow rain slicker.

"Sure looks like a body," the little girl said, trotting alongside the Appaloosa. She had wispy blond hair that stuck out from under her bonnet in tufts. Her little nose was wrinkled in thought. "And only kinda man I ever seen bring a body in under a slicker was a bounty hunter. There a big reward?"

A few townspeople stopped whatever they were doing to watch the grisly procession marching down Main Street. A couple of other children joined the little girl, gleefully tossing questions at Diamondback as if he were a circus performer.

"What'd he do?" she asked.

"Killed someone, I bet," a little boy in suspenders offered.

"Nah. Prob'bly just robbed a bank."

"They don't kill ya just for that."

"Sure they do," she explained. "Don't they, mister?"

Cord took a deep breath. He'd been riding for hours but still couldn't get the tart smell of smoke out of his lungs. Or that other heavier smell. Burnt flesh.

"Hey, you kids, get away there." A hatchet-faced woman in a ridiculous hat shooed the children away. "Get along now, Susie Perkins, 'fore I have your mama take a hairbrush to your backside. You too, Andy Horn. I'll be seein' you in school tomorrow. Get now."

The children scattered at her harsh schoolmistress voice, laughing as they ran into the alleys.

"Pardon me, ma'am," Diamondback asked her. "Tell me where I might find the sheriff?"

She studied him with a scornful frown, her eyes darting between him and the body folded across the horse. "End of the street," she said, pointing a gloved finger. "But he's outta town."

"Is there a deputy?"

"Ha. Not to my way of thinkin'." she sniffed, gathering her skirts and marching away.

Diamondback stared after her with a puzzled expression, then gently nudged his horse in the ribs. The second horse, with its terrible cargo, followed. They continued down the street, a morbid parade that caught everyone's eye.

He shifted in his saddle and grabbed the canteen hanging from the pommel, unfastened the cap and poured the rest of the cold water over his bandaged hands. As the water seeped through the torn ribbons of shirt he felt the wet coolness against his burns.

The first signs of dusk were starting to appear. Long grotesque shadows spilled across the dusty street. Shops were beginning to close. The noise from two saloons he passed was picking up a bit as the faro tables became crowded. Poisoned Well was a much larger town than Timberline. More stores. More people. More problems.

Cord moved lazily down the street, allowing the local residents to get a good look at him and his companion. Neither was in a hurry. He could have been here hours ago, of course, but for the cleaning up. After finding his horse, he'd gone back to retrieve his hat and his copy of *Ben-Hur*. Both were expensive. The horses from the buckboard hadn't gone too far, so they were no problem rounding up, though he'd kept only the stronger for this job. Then he'd gone back to the tree. And waited.

Waited while the last flames danced. Flickered. Then died. All the while he sat not twenty feet away, his dark eyes narrowed and unblinking, his copy of *Ben-Hur* balanced unopened on his knees. When it was over he waded through the smoldering ashes, shot the last few strands of barbed wire and bundled up the boy's fragile remains in his slicker. He could feel the dried bones cracking and shifting under even the gentlest pressure.

Then he headed into Poisoned Well.

The sheriff's office was an old wooden building at the far edge of town. It was in desperate need of whitewashing and the glass on the front window was cracked from a bullet hole in the center. From the amount of dirt caked onto the window, it looked to be an old wound.

The front door opened suddenly and the little blond girl in the blue sunbonnet dashed out, tugging a woman by the hand.

The woman was short, a couple inches over five feet, with straight black hair that cascaded over her shoulders down to her waist. She wore tight jeans tucked into leather boots with mule ears and a Starr double-action army .44 strapped to her narrow hips. She also wore a sheriff's star. She wasn't the first woman wearing a lawman's star that Diamondback had ever seen. But she was the first one who was also Chinese.

"That's him." The little girl pointed excitedly. "He's the bounty hunter we seen. Got a body there for sure."

Diamondback climbed down from his horse and stood in front of the petite woman. When she looked up at him, her eyes were almost as dark as his. They were calm, betraying no emotion.

"You the sheriff?" Cord asked.

"Acting sheriff," she explained without a trace of Chinese accent. That too was unusual. "The sheriff's taking a prisoner up to Reno. Be gone a few days."

The little girl in the sunbonnet yanked on the

woman's hand. "You gonna pay him the money now, Miss Tina?"

"We'll see, Susie. Now you go on back home. It'll be dark soon."

"Awww, I ain't afraid of the dark," the little girl complained, but marched off with furtive glances at them over her shoulder.

"Outlaw?" Miss Tina asked, nodding at the yellow slicker.

"I don't know."

She frowned. "Let's start with your name."

"Cord Diamondback."

"I'm Tina Jennings." She saw a flicker of surprise in his eyes. "What were you expecting, Mr. Diamondback? Chang? Wong? Ching? Jennings is my married name. The sheriff's my husband. Feel better?"

"Right now I don't feel much of anything."

"You a bounty hunter, Mr. Diamondback?" There was an edge of contempt in her voice.

"No."

"You kill him?"

"My bullet's in him, but I didn't exactly kill him."

"That's going to take some explaining, Mr. Diamondback."

And he did. Leaving out his encounters with Sheriff Tabor and Mrs. Scarf back in Timberline, he told her of the screams, the barbed wire, and the blazing fire, describing the young man's features with uncanny detail.

"Oh, my God," she gasped, her hand covering her mouth. "That's Silas DuBoir. Turned twenty-one last month. Nice kid."

"What was he doing with all that barbed wire?"

"He and his sister own a small spread out in Providence Valley. A bunch of small ranches out there, all stringing barbed wire to keep out the cattle from Gena Scarf's ranch. It's caused some trouble before, harsh words and vague threats, some shooting, but nothing like this. It's horrible."

"What are you going to do?"

She took a deep breath, flipped a layer of shimmering hair over her shoulder. "Guess I'll ride out and tell his sister, Lilith. See what she wants done with the body." She shook her head. "Now I know why my husband always considered this the worst part of his job."

"You want company?" Cord offered.

Suddenly her eyes flashed with defiance, her voice went cold. "I can handle my job, Mr. Diamondback."

"I never thought otherwise, Sheriff."

She stared into his eyes again, searching for something. The same contempt she usually found in whites, men in particular. But this time she found nothing. Finally her face relaxed and a weary smile played at her lips. "Sorry. Didn't mean to snap. You've already done a lot. I'm just a little touchy, is all. A lot of this town resent my husband for making me acting sheriff while he was gone, even though I'm a better shot than he is. Their only problem is that they don't know which to dislike more, the fact that I'm Chinese or that I'm a woman."

He smiled. "I guess there's more to being a good sheriff than shooting well."

She returned his smile. "So I've noticed. But no one else wanted the job who wasn't already allied with either Mrs. Scarf or the other ranchers. And the townspeople do business with both sides; therefore they wanted to stay neutral. So, I was the lucky one." She nodded at his bandaged hands. "In the meantime, let's get those burns tended to."

"Just point me to the doctor."

"I'll take you to him. He's pretty touchy about treating anybody after three o'clock. That's when he does his research."

"Thanks," he said, his dark eyes boring into hers.

She flushed, looked down, then took the lead, walking rapidly down the street. "Not too far," she said, her voice suddenly flat and businesslike.

Diamondback walked behind her, appreciating her slim figure. Her long black hair bounced against her back, flickering with red highlights from the setting sun.

"Right here," she said, turning the corner.

A small house with a neat little vegetable garden surrounding it stood behind a white picket fence. Cord noticed there were no weeds in the garden. A hand-painted sign hung around the front door, the letters drawn in ornate but precise letters: DO NOT DISTURB!

"Doesn't need the business?" Cord asked.

Tina Jennings shrugged. "He's retired. He only does the doctoring since our regular doctor moved back east. Just until we get another one out here. Mostly he likes to grow a lot of funny herbs and do research." She knocked on the front door. They waited but there was no answer.

"Maybe he isn't home," Cord suggested.

"He's home." She knocked again, louder. "It's me, Tina Jennings. Open up."

"Go away," the deep voice inside answered.

"I have a man who needs your help."

"Too bad."

"Come on, Doc. He's hurt."

"Life is cruel."

"So are you, you old toad."

A deep chuckle echoed from inside.

She smiled like a woman indulging a child. "Open up or no more discussions about Chinese medicinal herbs. Ever."

A long pause. "It's unlocked," the voice answered with defeat.

Tina Jennings opened the door and nodded for Cord to follow. Inside was a finely furnished living room, immaculately clean. Not a speck of dust in the whole room. Thick leather-bound books lined every wall from ceiling to floor.

"My husband brings me here every so often for lessons in housekeeping." She laughed. "Come on out, Doc. I have a patient for you."

"How nice for me," the voice grumbled. Then the owner of the voice came through the doorway, drying his hands with a towel. He was shorter even than Tina, perhaps less than five feet. His thick hair was snow-white and neatly combed, his spruce mustache was nothing more than a white line above full lips. Even the wrinkles in his face had a certain order and symmetry, as if he'd arranged them himself for maximum neatness. He was what the ladies would call dapper.

He looked up from his hands with an annoyed expression and stared at Diamondback. Suddenly his mouth dropped open and his eyes widened.

"My God," he whispered. *"Christopher Deacon!"*

Diamondback saw the sheriff reach for her gun.

7

"Christopher Deacon?" Tina scowled, snapping her gun out of the holster.

Diamondback remained perfectly still.

"Very good, Tina." Dr. Felix Goldhaven clapped his neatly manicured hands appreciatively. "Less than two seconds. But I'm sure you could have done better if it wasn't for your long hair. You probably don't notice, but you always do a little flip with your shoulder before—"

"Doctor, what about Christopher Deacon?"

"Oh, that." He chuckled. "I'm afraid that was just a little joke of mine. Not a joke really, a stimulus. A catalyst for—"

"What the hell are you talking about?"

"My experiment, of course. I was testing your reflexes for an experiment I'm conducting comparing male and female reaction times. Quite interesting differences. Controversial stuff, indeed. My findings are going to make a lot of people mad."

"Well, you've already made me mad." Tina Jennings frowned suspiciously, studying Cord's impassive face, then Dr. Goldhaven's jovial smile. Slowly she reholstered her gun. "I would've thought you'd know better, Doctor. That's one name you don't mention in fun, especially around lawmen. You're liable to get some innocent man shot." She looked at Diamondback.

"I apologize." Dr. Goldhaven bowed slightly. "But it required a strong shock to properly test you." He shrugged helplessly and looked at Cord. "As you can see, I'm without accurate scientific instruments and must conduct experiments under the most primitive conditions. Not easy times for a scientist."

Diamondback said nothing.

"But then you probably aren't interested in this academic sort of thing." He nodded at Cord's gun. "You've obviously developed other, uh, interests."

"Quite the contrary, Doctor," Diamondback said. "I'm quite appreciative of the unpredictable nature of your work. The examination of one thing can often lead to the discovery of something entirely different. Last year chemists Remsen and Fahlberg were investigating the oxidation of *o*-toluenesulfonamide and they discovered something called saccharin."

"Saccharin?" Tina asked, staring at Cord with awe. "What's that?"

"A nonnutritive sweetener five-hundred times stronger than sugar," Dr. Goldhaven explained, his eyes fixed on Diamondback. "Quite a boon for diabetics."

"I guess that's the point, Doctor. Things are not always what they seem in your work. You go looking for one thing, you find something else. But maybe that something else will be even better

Judgement at Poisoned Well

than your original goal. It's important to withhold judgements."

Dr. Goldhaven ran a finger lightly along the edge of his mustache. "You certainly seem well informed about science, sir. Unusual out here."

Diamondback smiled. "Science interests me."

"Well, not me." Tina Jennings sighed. "At least not tonight. I've got some bad work to do and I guess I've delayed it too long as is."

"What kind of bad work?"

She explained, recounting the incident as Cord had done for her.

"Horrible, horrible," Dr. Goldhaven said, shaking his head. "What kind of animals could do that?"

"That's what I'll be explaining to poor Silas's sister. In the meantime, take care of Mr. Diamondback for me, Doc. Burned and cut his hand on that damned barbed wire."

"Diamondback?" Dr. Goldhaven said, startled. "Cord Diamondback?"

"Yes."

"I've heard the name, sir." There was disapproval in his voice.

"You have?" Tina Jennings asked.

"Oh, yes, Tina. He's achieved a minor reputation as an informal arbitrator. Settles disputes for parties who wish to bypass the proper legal channels. Then enforces his, uh, rulings with violence when necessary. Is that an accurate description of your profession, Mr. Diamondback?"

"It'll do."

Tina lifted her eyes and stared directly into Cord's face. "I can't say I care much for that kind of work, Mr. Diamondback. But as long as you don't interfere with the law here in Poisoned Well, I can't complain. Besides, I figure we owe you some hospitality for trying to help Silas." She started toward the door. "Looks like you two will have plenty to talk about until I get back. Seems like you have some things in common, aside from an interest in science. Dr. Goldhaven is also an expert in the law. Used to teach it back east."

"Medicine and law," Cord said. "Interesting."

"To hear him tell it, anyway," she teased. But there was no humor in her expression. She was too preoccupied with her grisly mission. She waved her hand at them. "Be back in a few hours. You can check into the Deerlodge Hotel if you've a mind to stay for the night, Mr. Diamondback. They'll treat you right for a fair price. Doc can give you directions. Bye."

She hurried out the door.

The two men stood staring at each other for a while without movement or sound.

"So, Christopher," Dr. Goldhaven finally said with a sad shake of his immaculate head. "This is what's become of you?"

8

"Naturally, I'm disappointed."

Diamondback said nothing.

"We expected so much from you. Even more than from your brother. Hell, he was the first to admit you were the more talented one."

No reply.

"Here, let me see your hands." He led Cord into the back room where his medical equipment was laid out in neat measured rows. "I'm sorry about that slipup in there in front of Tina, Christopher. I mean, announcing your real name like that. Very stupid of me."

"It doesn't matter. You recovered well."

"It's just that you caught me by surprise. I haven't seen you in, what, six years? Since you left the university to visit Eric. After that all I knew was what I read in the newspapers." He began to unwrap the bloody strips of shirt. "Hmmm. Good medical work. Kept it clean and wet. I said you had the knack. Told your father you would have made a fine doctor."

"Instead of law?"

He shook his head. "In addition to law. Like me. Few doctors out here make a living just treating patients. Most have a sideline. Banking, politics, pharmacies. Fortunately I also have a law degree."

"A law degree." Cord laughed. "That's like saying the Pope preaches now and then. You're one of the most respected legal minds in the country, for Chrissakes. You taught at Harvard for twenty-five years—"

"Thirty."

"Thirty years, then. Not only that, but you are a renowned surgeon. What I want to know is what the devil are you doing in a Nevada town called Poisoned Well?"

"A little thing called retirement, my boy. Happens to the best of us."

"Not to you. I know you too well. And I know Harvard. They used your prestige to attract other faculty and funds. Even after retirement they would have stuffed and bronzed you rather than let you come out here. What's the real reason?"

Dr. Felix Goldhaven laughed, which suddenly turned into a hacking, coughing spasm. Diamondback rushed forward to help his old professor but was waved back.

"Asthma?"

"I wish," Dr. Goldhaven said, gasping for breath. His face was bright red. "Chronic pulmonary tuberculosis. The drier climate out here should prolong my life for another couple of years."

Diamondback looked at the short, stylish man, who once was his teacher, his brother's teacher and his father's teacher, and noticed for the first time how small he really was. There'd been some weight loss, but more telling was a grayishness to the skin that made him look a little tired. But there was still that arrogant sparkle in his eye, the driving curiosity to know everything about everything that had made him both respected and feared. Even as he'd announced his own impending death, there'd been no bitterness or fear. Merely a statement of fact, another adventure that he awaited with curiosity and skepticism.

"Enough of me," he said, fussing over Cord's hands with salve and bandages. "It's you that I want to know about." He stared at Cord with pale gray eyes, imbedded like jewels among the wrinkled folds of flesh. "I've heard awful things, Christopher. Now I want your side."

And Diamondback told him. Everything. How he'd left Harvard Law School after a year to visit his older brother in San Francisco. With both their parents dead, he'd come to rely more on his brother, despite their differences. Eric had always done the proper thing, followed in Father's impressive footsteps by attending Harvard Law School. But Christopher had never felt comfortable in those well-worn shoes. At sixteen he had rebelled against the Deacon formula and shipped off around the world on a whaler. When he'd come back, he learned of his parents sickness and death. Having no other plans, he'd allowed Eric to convince him to go back to school. After the first year of law studies, Christopher had felt the itch to travel again, and journeyed west to San Francisco, where Eric had built a small law practice. Unfortunately, his older brother had hooked into a case of opium smuggling, slave running, and a hundred other crimes that he'd traced back to the West's most popular politician, Senator Billy Fallows. Eric Deacon was close to uncovering the senator's involvement, but before that could happen, the two brothers were attacked in an alley. Eric was kidnapped, and Christopher, trying to protect his frailer brother, was slashed across the back a dozen times, the scars of which attack he still bore. Eric's bloated body, half eaten by fish, was pulled out of the bay a week later. But by then Christopher had hunted Senator Billy Fallows down, found him in bed with the wife of the mayor of San Francisco and made him confess to ordering Eric's murder. Then, with a strength that comes only from rage, he'd shoved a sharp New Bedford harpoon through the senator's stomach and out his spineless back.

"Since then I've changed my name a lot. Did a hitch in the cavalry. Changed my appearance, kept moving."

"Lord, Christopher." Dr. Goldhaven shook his head. "They shall never let you rest. Billy Fallows was worshiped by too many people. You would have been better off killing President Garfield. At least nobody likes him that much."

Diamondback shrugged.

"And now you're passing yourself off as a judge."

"I'm not passing myself off. I *am* a judge."

"Cord Diamondback?"

"Cord was my grandfather's name. Diamondback was a gift from the Shoshones for helping them. I like it."

"Such a waste, Christopher. You could have been anything. A real judge."

Cord smiled. "I am a real judge, Professor.

Judgement at Poisoned Well   73

Maybe not the kind you're used to. But real to the people who hire me."

"But the law—"

"The law as you know it—as you taught it—is a fine thing. In theory. But out here that theory doesn't always apply. Your law has been refined over centuries by a civilization. Out here civilization is far away. We haven't evolved that far yet. We're throwbacks to another time. You can't apply laws and methods designed for one group to another group. It doesn't work."

"So you take the law into your own hands. As you did in avenging Eric."

"Yes."

"I cannot approve, Christopher."

"I didn't ask for your approval, Professor."

Dr. Goldhaven looked hurt, his face sagging from his pupil's words.

Cord saw the pain on the old man's face, but said nothing. He had spoken the truth and it needed no defense.

"What are you doing here in Poisoned Well?" Dr. Goldhaven asked. "More of your judging?"

"Perhaps. I was offered a job by Mrs. Scarf."

"Gena Scarf? Very beautiful." He sighed with a lusty grin. "But very dangerous."

"That was my assessment."

"Did you accept her offer?"

"No. She wanted a hired gun. That's not what I do."

"Isn't it?"

They stared at each other a moment.

"Let's not argue about it, Professor," Cord said

finally. "We're not likely to change each other's minds."

"You still haven't answered my question. What are you doing here? Maybe I can't stop what you do other places. But this is my home now, and I'll not have you come here and inflict your homemade law on my home. I will not tolerate that, Christopher." His face burned red again and Cord was afraid he'd start another coughing spasm.

"Okay, it's your home. And what do you intend to do about the trouble that's going on here between Mrs. Scarf's people and the small ranchers in Providence Valley?"

"The law will take care of that," he said firmly.

"And Silas DuBoir?"

"The law will take care of that too."

Cord shook his head. "It's too late for that, Professor. She's out there hiring gunfighters. People who kill for a living. Within a couple days, this place will be a battleground. I've seen it happen before."

Dr. Goldhaven shook his head stubbornly. "The law—"

"The law can't do anything! One Chinese woman with a badge and a gun isn't going to stop a range war. No one person could."

"You mean no one person except you," he said sarcastically.

"That's right, Professor. Except me."

"And what makes you so goddamned special, Christopher?"

Diamondback smiled. "I'm the one with a plan."

Dr. Goldhaven glared at Cord for a moment, then waved a dismissing hand. "Plan, ha! What

Judgement at Poisoned Well 75

you do doesn't require a plan, just ammunition. I'll show you a plan." He led Cord back into the sitting room, pulled down a hefty volume and handed it to Cord.

Diamondback read out loud *"The Family Physician, or Domestic Medical Friend: Containing Plain and Practical Instructions for the Prevention and Cure of Diseases*. Catchy title."

"Isn't it. How about this gem?" He flipped another book out of the shelf and tossed it to Cord.

"The House Surgeon and Physician; Designed to Assist Heads of Families, Travelers, and Seafaring People. We had a copy of this aboard the whaler I shipped on. What's the point?"

"The point?" Dr. Goldhaven's pointed to another text in the shelves; *Gunn's Domestic Medicine, or Poor Man's Friend*. "The point, my dear Christopher Deacon or Cord Diamondback or whatever the hell name you're using, is that these are the major sources of medical treatment out here. The most popular is this last one, published in 1830 and still selling hundreds of thousands of copies. And all are hopelessly outdated. Worse, just plain wrong."

He strode across the room, his hand skimming his stylish white hair in search of any out-of-place strands. When he found none, he continued. "Just as you have your 'plan,' so do I have mine. To write a comprehensive medical text designed exclusively for the layman. Using not only the latest in medical knowledge, but also incorporating the ancient herbal medicine practiced by primitive tribes and foreign civilizations." His voice rose as his excitement grew. He began waving his hands as he explained. "People will be able to grow their own medicines right in their vegetable gardens. They will be able to diagnose ailments more accurately. They will—" He erupted into a sudden burst of coughing, much worse than the last. He sank to the davenport, gasping for air. Finally, his breathing shallow but controlled, he smiled at Cord. " 'Physician heal thyself,' eh, Christopher?"

"It's great work, Professor. Important work."

Dr. Goldhaven nodded weakly. "Naturally. That is the only kind of work I do. But time, Christopher, may prevent my completing this." He lifted his eyes to look at his former pupil. His face was still flushed from coughing, his eyes runny from the strain. "I could use help. Intelligent, educated help. Most importantly, *young* help."

The offer hung in the air. Diamondback shifted uncomfortably. "I'm sorry Professor. I appreciate the offer. But I can't. I have my own work."

"You compare what you do with *my* work?" He bristled.

Diamondback shrugged. "It's what I do."

"But you must see that—"

Heavy fists pounded against the front door.

"Dr. Goldhaven, you'd better hurry," a man called, though with no particular urgency.

Dr. Goldhaven marched over to the door and flung it open. "Damn it, Charles, you know better than to disturb me at this hour."

Charles nodded his skinny bald head and hitched his baggy pants. "Suit yourself, Doc, but I figured you'd want to be there to take care of the bodies."

"The bodies? Who's been hurt?"

Charles hitched his pants again and shrugged. "Nobody as yet. But the way it's goin, it won't be long now. I went to find the sheriff's missus, but she's gone who knows where. Laundry, prob'ly." He chuckled, hitched his pants.

"Who's involved?"

"A coupla Mrs. Scarf's boys. Simpson and Tyler. And some stranger. With the accent on *strange*." He shook his bald head and grinned. Four of his front teeth were missing. "Ain't never seen anything quite like this fella before. Some kinda artist," he said, posing grandly and twirling the end of an imaginary mustache. "Well, he's about to get his fancy ass shot off."

"That's not my concern," Dr. Goldhaven said.

Diamondback stood up. "This artist. He wear a big floppy hat and a long leather coat?"

"Yup."

"Kind of slim, about your height?"

Charles looked confused, hitched his pants. "Yeah, that's the fella."

Diamondback nodded at Dr. Goldhaven. "Grab your bag, Professor. You're going to have some work tonight." He turned to Charles and prodded him out the door. "Let's go, lead the way."

They trotted down the street, stopping once while Dr. Goldhaven struggled through another coughing fit. A few minutes later they quietly pushed through the bat-wing doors of Poisoned Well's Watering Hole Saloon. No one much noticed them. Everyone's attention was on the two blustering men at the bar and the quiet man they were addressing.

"Tell me something, Tyler." Simpson was speaking, his voice slurred. "You ever seen anything more ridiculous in your life? I mean, look at that hat. He looks like my damn sister."

"Nah." Tyler shook his head sagely. "Your sister's got more of a mustache."

The two men slapped each other as they laughed. A few of the other patrons chuckled, but most just stood silent. Waiting.

The man they were addressing sat alone at a table, a full glass of beer next to him. His feet were propped up on a chair and leaning against his knees was a large sketch pad. He was drawing something on the pad with a thin stick of charcoal. He paid no attention to Simpson and Tyler, which was making them angrier.

"I think maybe I ought to send that hat to my sister," Simpson said, his voice tight, his body hunched for action. " 'Cept I seen that same thing on a whore once in Carson's Pass. Whore was so old I wouldn't spit on her, let alone stick anything of mine in her."

"Maybe that's where this gent got that hat." Tyler suggested, taking the same menacing pose as his buddy. "Maybe that whore was his mother."

Diamondback sighed. "Well, Professor, forget what I said about my little plan. All bets are off. Someone's just slipped a joker into the deck." He nodded at the man with the sketch pad.

"You know that man?"

"Know him?" Diamondback smiled wryly. "I'm the one who killed him."

9

"You know what I'm thinkin', Tyler?"

"No, what're you thinkin'?"

"I'm thinkin' that, whore's hat or not, I want it."

"What for? It don't go with any of your clothes."

"Not for me." Simpson guffawed, playfully punching Tyler in the arm. "To send to my little sister in Houston."

Tyler scratched his stubbled chin with mock concern. "Well, now, Simpson, how the devil do you figure to get a hat like that?"

"You didn't hear me, Tyler," Simpson said, a cruel grin slitting his face. "I don't want a hat *like* that. I want *that* hat. Now that I think about it, I believe I did let my horse fuck that old whore in Carson's Pass. So it's got sentimental value now."

Diamondback began to slowly weave his way around behind the fringe of the crowd.

"Hey, Mr. Artist," Simpson drawled, stepping away from the bar, his right hand brushing the edge of his holster.

The man at the table still did not look up. He

sketched with rapid strokes, his lips moving slightly as if he were singing to himself. But the only sound in the room now was the scratching of his charcoal across the sketch pad.

Simpson winked at Tyler, then took another step forward. "You deaf, Mr. Artist? You got paint in your ear or somethin'?"

"Maybe he's too scared to speak?" Tyler offered, tappin a dirty fingernail against his beer mug.

"Yeah." Simpson nodded and took another step forward. The crowd circling the scene backed up a few steps as they hastily calculated which way the bullets might fly.

Diamondback squeezed quietly past a few men, easing himself to the front of the crowd until he stood directly behind the stranger. He had to be certain, sure there was no mistake as to who this stranger was. But standing this close to him again, he knew it was true. It was *him*. Cord said nothing, did nothing. Merely waited for the inevitable.

Simpson, sensing that the crowd was growing restless with this game, decided to step up the action. He swaggered over to the table and loomed directly in front of the man.

But the artist continued to sketch, cocking his head to the right than left, alternately frowning and smiling at his work. Ignoring Simpson.

"Get up," Simpson growled in a low voice. Tyler moved to the right, let his hand drop next to his gun.

The artist squinted at his pad, leaned forward to draw some detail work. But did not look up.

Suddenly Simpson kicked over the chair that had propped up the artist's feet. The pad jerked

Judgement at Poisoned Well 81

off the man's knees and his charcoal skidded across the paper.

"I said for you to get up."

The man shrugged. "Okay. But you're not going to like that black line across your forehead."

"Huh?"

The artist handed him the sketch pad. Simpson stared at it, his mouth open, his face pinched with shock. Tyler shuffled forward to look over Simpson's shoulder. His face drained to a pale shade.

It was a magnificent drawing. Every tiny detail of the saloon was there. The large mirror behind the bar with its ornate frame of twining snakes. The various bottles stacked behind the bar, even their labels. The bartender, Abel Rawlings, was there, his bushy black longhorn mustache gleaming in the dim light. And you could even see his back reflected in the bar mirror, the shaggy hair brushing the collar.

But then there was the strange part. The shocking part. Sprawled out in front of the bar were two crumpled bodies, their eyes closed in clenched death masks. Their faces twisted with agony, yet still familiar.

Simpson and Tyler.

Simpson's stomach was dark with blood, his pants wet with excrement. His gun was still in its holster, though his dead hand was wrapped limply around it. Tyler lay propped against the bar, a bloody hole gaping in his chest. His gun was also still in its holster. It was Simpson and Tyler all right, every detail clear. Simpson's hand-tooled holster, which he'd bought in Mexico from a kid who'd stripped it off a gringo who had died the night before of a rattlesnake bite. And Tyler's shirt with the tiny Statues of Liberty all over it, that his niece had sent to him from Chicago. But the faces were slightly different. There was no mistaking who they were, yet Simpson's face had the subtle but obvious characteristics of a rat to it. Sharp and beady. Tyler's looked more furtive, like a squirrel.

But both were unmistakably dead.

"Get up!" Simpson barked, throwing the sketch pad onto the table. It slid against the full mug, splashing a few drops of beer onto the drawing. The charcoal bled.

"Not much of an art lover, eh?" the artist said, rising. He wasn't tall. He stood an inch or two under Simpson, an inch or two over Tyler. He removed his floppy hat with a flourish and dropped it on the chair behind him. Without his hat, he looked to be barely thirty, with sandy hair that hung over his collar. He had a long mustache, but it was even lighter colored than his hair and was therefore not very noticeable. His face was thin and handsome, though his features were delicate, almost fragile. Several in the crowd thought they detected a slight accent, though none could properly identify it.

The artist shrugged out of his heavy leather coat. Despite the heat, he wore a long black jacket beneath it, as well as a white shirt and a string tie. He also wore two guns, one on each hip in separate crossing holsters. The guns were Peacemaker .45s with the front of the trigger guards cut away for easier access. Attached to each holster was a short flat throwing knife.

The crowd muttered loudly about this new

development, arguing freely about the outcome. A few cash bets were made.

Sweat bloomed across Simpson and Tyler's foreheads. Simpson licked dry lips. Tyler swallowed something hard.

"Well, I'm up," the artist said good-naturedly. "Now what?"

Simpson looked confused for a moment, as if he didn't understand the question. Then a few onlookers chuckled softly and he remembered. He took a deep breath, drawing himself up, letting his lips curl into a snarl. "You tryin' to be funny with that drawing?"

"Not at all. Do you see anything funny in it?"

Simpson glanced nervously around the room. Hard curious eyes stared back. It was his move. He pointed at the drawing. "You made me look like a rat or somethin'."

The artist shrugged. "Beauty is in the eye of the beholder."

A few more chuckles.

Simpson hunched his shoulders, letting his hands drop to his holster. Slowly he started to back up. "Well see." He nodded at the artist's guns. "Anytime you're ready, Mr. Artist. Two guns don't scare us. Right, Tyler?"

Tyler sighed, swallowing that same stubborn lump. "Maybe we should just forget it, Steve. It ain't worth it. We got a job to do for Mrs. Scarf. She told us not to get into any trouble with the townspeople."

"He ain't no townspeople. He's a stranger."

"Still, it ain't worth it. Let it go."

The artist nodded. "Listen to your friend."

"Shut up!" Simpson spun on Tyler with a sneer. "I ain't askin' you to back me. You're turnin' to duck piss in front of my eyes, that's your problem. Only after I nail him, I don't want you ridin' with me again. Ever."

Tyler sighed again, a heavy breath of defeat. "I didn't say I wasn't backin' you." He squared off next to his friend, his hand twitching next to his gun.

"Loyalty's a good thing," the artist said to Tyler. He picked up a piece of charcoal and hovered over his sketch a moment. "I'm going to take that into consideration."

It took only a few strokes, but when he showed the drawing again, the image of Tyler no longer had a bullet through his heart. It was a couple inches to the left, in the shoulder. And the eyes were open now, in pain, but definitely alive. The artist laughed, dropped the sketch on the table. "Well, boys?"

Diamondback folded his arms and stepped back.

Simpson was the first to move. His hand slapped at his gun with a clean practiced movement. His body was already turning into a protective crouch.

Tyler was only a fraction of a second slower, his nervous hand a little more tentative.

But it didn't matter.

The artist drew both guns and fired before either man had cleared leather. The sound of both guns firing at once was loud, and Simpson wondered what that noise could be just as he felt the first bullet tear through his stomach. The pain was much greater than he'd ever imagined it would be. He had a sudden image of a wolverine gnawing its way through his guts and out his back, its fur matted with wet blood. By the time the second and third bullets mashed his intestines into a slushing pulp, he was already dead. He dropped to the floor, his eyes closed, his dead hand limply gripping his still-holstered gun.

Tyler didn't hear the explosions at all. He was busy cursing Simpson for getting him in this fix. He knew they'd lost before the artist had even pulled the trigger. He'd looked up and seen the two guns flying out of their crossed holsters like attacking hawks. He'd felt his own hand still tugging his Colt out of the holster. And he'd known. Then he felt the razor pain in his shoulder, saw the spray of blood where the bullet punched through a tiny Statue of Liberty, and felt himself sag to the floor, his shoulder shattered, his arm numb and bleeding.

"Lookit that," one of the onlookers called out. "Dropped 'em just like in his drawing. Goddamn!"

Burly, sweaty men crowded around, passing the drawing among themselves, discussing the probabilities. Shaking their heads.

"Get out of the way, you morons," Dr. Goldhaven grumbled, shoving his way through the crowd toward Tyler. He used his black medical bag to prod them aside.

The artist draped his leather coat over his shoulders and fixed his hat on his head at a properly rakish angle. He started toward the door. Everybody avoided him. Everybody except one.

"Duncan Toth."

He heard his name behind him, recognized the voice. He turned, his hands dropping to his guns. "Cord Diamondback," he said with a thin smile. "I suppose you know. You're next."

10

"What's it like to be dead?"

"It has certain advantages."

"Like no one following you?"

Duncan Toth shrugged. "It does cut down on your circle of acquaintances."

"Especially relatives of men you've killed."

"Nuisances."

"Sounds ideal," Cord said.

"Not ideal. But safe."

"And boring?"

Toth laughed. "Restful."

Diamondback entered the sheriff's office, glanced around to make sure the cells were empty, waved Toth in. With Dr. Goldhaven still busily tending Tyler's wounded shoulder in the saloon, this was the only place they could agree on where they could talk privately.

They had a lot to say. But they said most of it with their eyes.

Diamondback unstrapped his holster and hung it on the hat hook in the corner before pulling up a chair and sitting.

Toth chuckled, tossing his floppy hat onto the sheriff's desk as he sprawled back into the sheriff's chair and propped up his feet. He nodded at the holster. "Getting cautious, Cord?"

"I don't want there to be any mistakes, that's all. I didn't come here to shoot it out with you."

Toth's laugh was a harsh rasp. "Because you know goddamn well I'm faster than you."

"Yes."

Toth leaned forward in his chair, his face suddenly tight, his mouth a thin slit. "That didn't seem to matter last year in Faraday County. You still managed to pump three bullets in me and get away without a scratch."

"Not quite without a scratch. One of your shots cracked a rib."

"I didn't know." Toth grinned. "It doesn't make me feel any better."

"Me neither."

There was a moment of silence while each man evaluated the other. Diamondback didn't like sitting there without his gun, didn't like the vulnerability. But it was the only way to control the situation. Toth was unpredictable, capable of sudden explosions of raw emotion. Violence. If Cord had kept his gun on, anything might have set Toth reaching for his. He was only waiting for an excuse to avenge their showdown last year. But Cord wanted to avoid that. Especially since Toth was the faster of the two.

"I see you're wearing two guns now."

Toth patted his left holster. "Yeah, pretty aren't they. A little lesson I learned from you." His blue eyes rolled back slightly as if he were looking directly into the past. "Last year you beat me out of cleverness, not speed. You made me chase you, waste most of my bullets. Then you maneuvered me around that ghost town like a pet dog, popping out on my left side so I had to spin to fire. And you had the damned morning sun at your back. That's how you managed to almost kill me."

"Almost? You looked dead from where I was standing. Your eyes were open and you weren't breathing."

Toth grinned again, a row of small even teeth blossoming from between thick red lips. "I've learned a few tricks myself over the years."

Cord nodded, silently cursing himself for not having checked the pulse, or at least firing a couple more cleanup shots into the body when he'd had the chance.

"Yeah, you should have checked," Toth continued, knowing Cord's thoughts. "But you were in a hurry to rush off and be the hero. Anyway, it was a good lesson for me, almost a fatal one. I spent the next year in hibernation, practicing with my left hand. For one whole year I didn't even use my right hand. I ate, drank, shaved, screwed—everything with my left hand. Now I'm as fast with my left as I am with my right." He leaned forward again, his blue eyes wide and sparkling. "Now I don't have a blind side."

Suddenly he bolted upright, his left hand slapping at his holster, his arm lashing with a blur. A sharp whistle sliced by Diamondback's ear. The sound behind him was a thud followed by a clink. He glanced over his shoulder. One of Toth's flat throwing knives was sticking out of Cord's holster.

Toth chuckled. "Not bad, huh?"

Diamondback shook his head. "That's a twenty-dollar holster you just ruined."

"What?" Toth frowned angrily.

"Twenty dollars. Not counting all the time it took breaking in."

"What are you saying?"

"I'm saying that I don't intend to walk around with a holster that has a knife hole in it. Looks sloppy. That's bad for business. You owe me twenty dollars."

Toth's full lips took on a pouting look as he chewed the inside of his cheek. He pushed his chair back from the desk and allowed both hands to drop near his guns. "And if I don't pay?"

Cord shrugged. "I hadn't thought about that."

"Think about it now." His face was grim, challenging.

"Well, then." Cord sighed. "I suppose I'll have to sue you for it in court."

Duncan Toth looked confused at first, but slowly, almost against his will, his mouth stretched into a broad grin and he found himself laughing. "Sue me, eh? Well, I wouldn't want that." He reached into his pocket, pulled out a handful of coins, selected a twenty-dollar goldpiece and tossed it to Cord.

Cord studied it carefully, sank his teeth into the soft edge. "You still getting paid in gold?"

"A small idiosyncrasy. But this is a troubled economy."

Cord pocketed the coin. He stood up, walked over to his holster, plucked the knife from the thick leather and returned to his chair. Leaning forward, he lofted the knife on top of Toth's floppy hat. It landed with a muffled thud.

"Now, Toth, what are you doing here?"

The heavy clomping of boots and loud muttering outside startled both men as they coiled their bodies for possible action.

"I'm making plenty of noise out here," Dr. Goldhaven's voice grumbled through the door. "So don't get trigger-happy and shoot me. I'm coming in, all right?"

Duncan Toth glanced at Diamondback, who nodded. Toth said, "Come ahead."

"Goddamned right I'll come ahead," Dr. Goldhaven said, flinging open the door and marching in. "I spent the last twenty minutes cleaning up after your mess, son. You owe me money."

"I didn't ask you to help that cowboy. That was your idea."

"That was my *duty*. In this case, one that I did grudgingly. Nevertheless, you were responsible, therefore you will pay my fee."

Toth held up his hands in surrender. "How much?"

"Two dollars."

Toth slid two silver dollars across the desk. "This is the most money-hungry town I've ever been in. I should fit in just fine."

"Which brings us back to my question," Cord said. "What are you doing here?"

"The same thing you are. Looking for work. I heard that the boss lady at the Rocking S was looking for some experienced men to help out around here with some nasty wire."

"Another gunman." Dr. Goldhaven sighed disgustedly, smoothing back his white hair.

"Not just another gunman," Diamondback explained. "One of the most ruthless, cold-blooded, double-crossing killers in the country."

Toth grinned. "Modesty prevents me from agreeing."

"And honesty prevents you from disagreeing. I know this man, Professor. He finds a conflict somewhere and forces it to violence."

"There's nothing for you around her, Toth. Strictly small potatoes," Dr. Goldhaven said.

"Small potatoes can grow into big potatoes."

"Don't pull any of your tricks around here."

"There's more money to be made when bullets are flying," Toth said.

"What tricks?" Dr. Goldhaven asked.

"Bad ones," Cord said. "First he takes a small conflict, forces it into something bigger, then he secretly goes back and forth between the opposing sides and sells his services to both of them."

"Whoa there, Diamondback. You get paid by both sides too."

"To ensure impartiality. And to *stop* a fight, not escalate it." Cord turned to Dr. Goldhaven. "What happened in the saloon tonight—he started it."

"Now just a minute, Cord," Dr. Goldhaven said. "Maybe you're right about this man's character, I don't know. But not about what happened in the saloon. I was there too. Those men, Simpson and Tyler, they started it. They were the ones threatening him."

"That's right, Diamondback. Pay attention to the doc."

"They were suckered, Professor. I've seen him work before, it's part of his style. Toth rides into a town where he knows the action is heating up. He finds a couple men from one side, doesn't matter which. He gets them to pick a fight. Like tonight, he probably walked into the saloon, 'accidentally' bumped into one of them as he passed by, apologized profusely, then sat at the table nearest them. If they hadn't noticed his strange clothes before, they did then."

Toth looked hurt. "I always thought you liked my clothes," Toth said.

"He sat in front of them and started to sketch them. Anything to make them feel uneasy. With men like Simpson and Tyler it's easy to get them to start something. But it always ends the same way, with one or both of them dead. They didn't stand a chance."

"But why?" Dr. Goldhaven asked. "What's the point?"

"Advertising. Now both sides know he's here and what he can do. By tomorrow, one of them will probably make him an offer. He'll accept, then go to the other side and try to sell them out. Back and forth, each time extracting more money."

Toth shrugged. "It does get confusing."

"It must," Dr. Goldhaven said. "Never knowing whose side you're on."

"Oh, I always know whose side I'm on." He smiled. "Mine."

"The drawings," Cord said. "You've gotten better."

"Think so? My mother was quite a painter, you

know, taught me how to draw as a child. I just never had much use for it before now."

"She must be proud of the way you've utilized her teaching," Dr. Goldhaven said.

"She doesn't complain. Hasn't since she died eight years ago. Besides, I think she'd get a kick out of it. She always wanted me to be an artist. And I've become one. I struggle for proper composition in whatever I do, whether it's drawing a picture . . . or drawing a gun." He stood up, skidding the chair behind him. Slowly he slid his knife back into the sheath on the holster, then adjusted his floppy hat at just the right angle. He smiled broadly. "Well, so much for catching up on old times. I guess we have each other straight now, Diamondback. No harm in admitting that, although I came here to make money, I figured you might be here too. This isn't the first place I looked. Your reputation has grown in certain professional circles in the past year. Almost to where mine was . . . before my, uh, vacation. It's time I let everybody know I'm back in business. In a big way. You understand?"

Diamondback nodded. "I understand."

Toth smiled. "Good. Now, where's a good place to stay?"

Diamondback hooked a thumb over his shoulder. "I hear the Deerlodge Hotel is reasonable."

"Thanks." He saluted with two fingers and walked out the door.

Dr. Goldhaven turned to Cord with a puzzled expression. "Am I wrong, or did that man just threaten to kill you?"

"You're not wrong."

"And then you suggest a hotel for him to stay?"

"Isn't it a good hotel?"

Dr. Goldhaven threw up his hands in frustration. "He said he'd kill you, for God's sake. Don't be flip with me about it."

"Sorry, Professor. There's no point in getting upset. It's my own fault for not finishing him off when I had the chance."

"My God, Christopher, I thought I knew you. But this man sitting here talking about killing and finishing people off, I don't know him at all. And I don't want to know him." Cord noticed a flicker of moisture in the old professor's eyes as he grabbed his black medical bag and marched out, slamming the front door behind him.

Cord leaned back into his chair, propped his feet onto the sheriff's desk and considered his options. He could—probably should—ride away. Leave Poisoned Well to Gena Scarf, the ranchers of Providence Valley, Duncan Toth, Tina Jennings and Professor Goldhaven. Let them divide it any way they chose. After all, what did it matter to him? He didn't even have a client!

He shook his head. No good. He'd have to face Toth sooner or later. Now was as good a time as any. He'd have to be careful, that's all. Toth was faster, both with a gun and a knife. And now that he was packing twins he'd be twice as deadly.

But there was Professor Goldhaven. Dying, desperately hurrying to finish his book before it was too late. Poisoned Well was Goldhaven's home now, and he wanted it to be orderly, peaceful and law-abiding. The kind of society he'd spent his life trying to create. That was reason number two to stay.

And reason number three . . .

Diamondback heard the riders clomping up to the hitching post outside. At least a dozen horses. Tina Jennings' pleasant voice drifted in and he rose to meet her. He opened the front door just as she was leading a small group toward the office.

She looked startled, stepping backward. "Mr. Diamondback—"

"Diamondback?" one of the voices hollered hysterically. "He's the one! He's the murderer!"

In an instant, Cord Diamondback felt the two hands clutching at his throat, trying to squeeze the life out of him.

11

"Danny! Stop it, Danny!"

Danny ignored the woman's voice, lunging his body against Diamondback, knocking them both into the flimsy wall of the sheriff's office. Dried paint chips snowed onto their heads. The dirty window with the old bullet hole rattled, then shattered.

"Danny!" the woman shouted again, tugging at his arm.

Cord felt long bony fingers tightening, pressing against his windpipe, felt the hot breath of hate in his face. But he stayed calm. He moved slowly, deliberately, not wanting anybody to get hurt. Danny was only a boy, sixteen at most, and his delicate fingers were no match for the hard muscles in Cord's neck.

Gently Cord reached up and grabbed the thin wrists, twisting them outward until the boy's grasp was broken. Still Danny snarled at him, straining forward and snapping his teeth like a rabid mongrel. Saliva sprayed into Cord's face.

Tina Jennings and the other woman grappled

with the writhing boy, each snagging an arm and pulling him backward.

"Danny!" Tina said firmly.

"He killed Silas!" Danny screamed, tears sliding down his cheeks, mucus dripping from his nose. "He shot my brother!"

"No, Danny," the young woman pulling Danny's left arm said in a silky, soothing voice. "He injured himself trying to save Silas. When he saw he couldn't, he saved him from any more of that wretched pain. Silas would thank him if he could."

Danny shook his head violently. "He was there! He could have saved him!"

"He tried, Danny. Look at his hands. Look."

Danny stared at the bandages on Cord's hands. He calmed some, but didn't look totally convinced.

The young woman pulled out a handkerchief and dabbed at his eyes and nose.

"I'll take him over to the hotel," Tina Jennings said, pulling Danny away. "Nate will fix him something to eat."

Danny jerked his arm free. "I'm not hungry. I'm not ... ." He choked out a sob.

"I know, Danny. I know." They walked away and Tina Jennings glanced at Cord over her shoulder with an expression that said to take care of things until she got back.

Standing in a ragged bunch behind the young girl were ten men that had had ridden into town with Tina Jennings. Each was dressed in the same plain hand-sewn clothing. Each was heavily armed with a double-barreled shotgun, a pistol and a hunting knife. Each wore a grim scowl behind identical beards and their eyes searched the streets for enemies.

Behind them a dozen or so townspeople had gathered to point and stare and shake their heads.

"Maybe we'd better step into the sheriff's office," Cord suggested.

Silently the ten men and the girl followed him inside, the men fanning out with backs pressed against the walls, their shotguns cradled handily in their arms. The girl stood in the middle of the room and faced Cord.

She was probably a few months past twenty, and she stood erect and solemn, as if to show she could remain in control despite her terrible grief. Cord knew that such control usually came with practice at dealing with misfortune. And from the way she stood she must have had a lot of practice.

Cord lingered on her remarkable looks, the way all men and most women who saw her did. She had a kind of startling beauty. Her fine strawberry blond hair shimmered like corn silk. Her face was a perfect oval, the chin slightly pointed. She was so pretty it was disturbing. The kind of pretty that could make men instantly dissatisfied with what they thought was a happy life. They could see in her smooth features and graceful strength the possibilities for things better, richer than they knew. Perhaps that explained why many women hated her on sight.

As if aware of her power to arouse such feelings, and uncomfortably so, she seemed to do everything to hide her beauty. Her hair was pulled back into a tight matronly bun. Her sleek figure was draped in a long shapeless dress made from the same rough drab material as the men's clothing. But nothing could hide the small full lips, the robin's-egg eyes, the long delicate neck.

"I'm Lilith DuBoir," she said softly, sticking out her hand.

"Cord Diamondback," he said, surprised at the strength in her thin hand as they shook. Because of the bandages only his fingers touched her skin, but the cool sensation was thrilling.

"First, sir, let me apologize for my brother Danny. He and Silas were quite close, and we only just received the news. He's young and has not yet learned to control himself." A tear shone in her eye and she quickly wiped it away.

"No need to apologize, Miss DeBoir. I understand his feelings."

"You are generous, Mr. Diamondback." She nodded at his bandaged hands. "And terribly brave to have risked your own life to help my brother. We all appreciate it . . . deeply."

"Are you all family?" Cord asked, gesturing at the armed men behind her.

She smiled shyly. "Yes. One family under God."

"I see."

"Don't worry, Mr. Diamondback; although we are devoted followers, we aren't going to throw ourselves into spasms of prayer on the floor of the sheriff's office."

"I didn't think you would."

"Didn't you?" She smiled again. "Most people in this town seem to expect that sort of behavior from us because of our strict adherence to the Word. They think we do nothing but shout 'amen' to each other. They think—" Her voice had risen and she cut herself off abruptly, shrugging. "Anyway we are still a family, though out of choice rather than by blood. We were having our Bible meeting when Sheriff Jennings arrived with the news. These men insisted on guarding me on the ride into town."

"Those animals of Gena Scarf will stop at nothing," one of the men said. "I warned you before, Lilith; now you know for certain." He stepped away from the wall, gripping his shotgun as if he were controlling a need to shoot it. He was in his early thirties and had a thin white scar that started at the corner of his right eye and hooked down until it disappeared into his thick bushy beard.

"Well, you were right, Joseph." Lilith sighed. "Perhaps we were a little naive in our dealings with Mrs. Scarf. But it is our way to first try the peaceful solution. We shan't make that mistake again."

The front door opened and Tina Jennings stepped in. "I heard that, Lilith," she said. "And I don't want you or any of you other Providence Valley ranchers to start anything until I've conducted my investigation. We don't know for certain it was Gena Scarf's boys that done this."

"The hell we don't," Joseph barked.

"Joseph," Lilith scolded. "We don't speak such language, do we?"

He hesitated, then stepped back against the wall, clutching his shotgun even tighter.

Lilith turned to Tina, who stood several inches shorter than she. "Of course we won't take any action, Sheriff. But we will not allow ourselves to be slaughtered. The Bible says we have a right to protect ourselves, and we shall exercise that right."

"Well, the law and the Bible agree on that,"

Tina said. "But don't get overzealous about it, understand?"

"Tomorrow we'll be stringing new barbed-wire fences on our land. That too is our right. We wish no one harm, but if anyone tries to stop us, I swear that we shall hunt them down and kill them in the same way they killed Silas." Her voice vibrated slightly with the last part of her speech, and Cord could see the ragged edge of emotion peeking through her controlled surface.

"Just don't go hunting them on Gena Scarf's land," Tina warned. " 'Cause then you'll be in the wrong and I'll have to come out after you."

Lilith ignored Tina, turned to Cord. "Again, thank you for what you did for Silas. I know it couldn't have been easy for you. If there's anything we can do, please ask." She started toward the door.

"There is," Cord said.

She turned back, confused. "What?"

"There is something you can do."

She eyed him suspiciously. "Such as?"

"Give me a chance to stop this quarrel before it becomes a full-scale war."

Joseph hefted his shotgun. "It's too late for that now. They've made it a war already."

"And how would you stop it, Mr. Diamondback?"

"Negotiation."

"How would you get both sides to agree?"

"That's my problem."

She tilted her head, laid a finger against her lips. "But why place yourself in the middle of this conflict, Mr. Diamondback. It's not your fight and you could get killed. What do you get out of it?"

Judgement at Poisoned Well

"Money," he said flatly.

"That's all?"

"That's all. It's my profession to settle arguments like this. You pay me a fee and Mrs. Scarf pays me the same fee. Then I decide the fairest way to end this mess. I have references you can wire."

"And what happens"—Joseph sneered—"if when we hear your decision, we chose not to go along?"

Cord's dark eyes narrowed. "You will."

Joseph frowned, looked into Diamondback's dark eyes, swallowed hard.

Lilith shook her head. "I don't know, Mr. Diamondback. We're used to settling our own affairs, according to the laws of the Bible."

"And look what it's gotten you so far."

She bristled. "That was cruel, Mr. Diamondback."

"Perhaps. But things are only going to get worse around here. And you're going to let it. That's also cruel." He watched her wipe another tear away, struggle to keep her jaw from quivering. He took a deep breath, blew it out slowly. "If I could speak to your parents—"

"My parents are dead. Died on the trip out here. Fever."

"We all look after each other in Providence Valley," Joseph said, with something of a warning in his voice. "*We're* her family now."

Cord nodded. "Well, then, let me come out and speak to your people tomorrow night. You gather them all together and I'll explain my services. If you aren't interested, that will end it."

"We can save you the trip," Joseph said. "We aren't interested."

Cord ignored him, staring at Lilith. She nibbled on her lower lip, thinking. Finally she shrugged. "Although we don't encourage visitors to Providence Valley, Mr. Diamondback, we are in your debt. Therefore I shall do as you request. But I caution you, I agree with Joseph that you are wasting your time."

"It wouldn't be the first time."

Lilith turned toward the door. Her solemn friends encircled her, funneling after her through the door.

"Danny's over at the Deerlodge with Nate," Tina called after them. "He should feel a little better by now."

"Thank you, Sheriff," she said. "Lord bless you both."

Tina closed the door and shook her head. "It looks pretty bad. I'll be damned surprised if a couple people from both sides aren't killed tomorrow. Christ, I wish my husband were back."

"Well, maybe I can do something before the violence gets any worse."

"For a fee, of course." She frowned.

"Judging is my profession, Sheriff. I don't stick my nose into other people's business because I'm some noble do-gooder. I do it because the work is interesting and pays well."

"Like Duncan Toth?"

He raised an eyebrow. "You've heard?"

"Nate, the cook over at the Deerlodge Hotel, told me what happened at the saloon. Simpson's dead and Tyler's shoulder is shattered. But nothing I can charge Toth with." She flipped a curtain of black hair over her shoulder. Her thin lips smiled. "He a friend of yours?"

"The competition."

"I heard he was dead."

"Me too." Cord didn't show his displeasure over the fact that she'd heard of Duncan Toth but not Cord Diamondback. This was more Toth's part of the country, and his style had always been more flamboyant—and destructive. Besides, Cord had earned enough infamy under another name.

Tina Jennings slid an arm through his and guided him toward the door. "Streets can be dangerous this time of night. I'll walk you back to your hotel."

"A pleasant offer." He smiled. "If I didn't suspect you just wanted to make sure you knew where I was for the rest of the night."

"Maybe. With you and Duncan Toth tucked away, I can try to get a good night's sleep. Starting tomorrow there'll be very little sleep for anybody."

She blew out the lamps and locked the door behind them, slipping out of his arm the moment they were in the street. He smelled lavender perfume that she hadn't had on before she'd taken Danny to the hotel.

"Lilith DuBoir is a tough woman," he said.

"She's had to be. Lost her parents in Kansas but continued on out with her two brothers to claim the land her daddy'd bought in Providence Valley." She flipped her black hair over her shoulder and looked up into his face. "Don't tell me her toughness is the only thing about her you noticed."

He grinned. "She's beautiful."

"And then some. Isn't a man in town who doesn't dream of dumping his wife and running away with

Lilith. That hasn't made her very popular around here. The men resent that they can't have her and the women resent that she exists. Throw in that whole group's holier-than-thou attitude, and you have a hostile town."

"It's always been that way with religious people. Mormons, Jews, Christians. I guess people don't like to be reminded how sinful the rest of us are."

"Speak for yourself, Diamondback." She laughed. "Maybe you're right. They certainly don't mingle with the people around here much. They come to town only for business, to buy supplies or sell something. The rest of the time they stay out there in Providence Valley. They've even built their own church. That's one of the things that riled the folks around here so much. Made it seem like they was too good to pray in our church."

"Are all the ranchers in Providence Valley members of the same clan?"

She nodded. "Didn't start that way; a few came in and bought the land. Then they sent word to some friends back east. And their friends sent back for others. And soon they'd bought the whole valley. I guess it's hard for people like that to find a place where they can live their lives the way they want."

"And aside from some disapproval, the townspeople have left them pretty much alone?"

"Pretty much. There's been some teasing by the kids and a couple isolated incidents. But nothing much. The people of Poisoned Well need business to stay alive. They're not about to chase off any paying customers. That's one of the reasons they've not taken either side in this fight."

They reached the hotel. Cord looked it over and sighed. "Well, it's a step up from the Timberline Hotel, but not much."

She looked surprised. "You stayed at the Timberline?"

"A few nights ago."

"You have a bath?"

"Sort of."

"Then you met the old Chinese man who fills the tubs."

"Sure."

"How was he?"

Cord shrugged. "Seemed healthy enough, but didn't say much. Why, you know him?"

"Sort of. He's my father."

"Your father?" Remembering his various activities in Timberline, Cord experienced a moment of anxiety and asked, "Does he write often?"

"Not much."

Cord relaxed. "If he could only see you now."

She shook her head. "If he knew what I was doing he'd kill me. Very unladylike to be a sheriff, even an acting one. Very un-Chinese."

Cord turned and looked down at her, his dark eyes locked on hers, squeezing them as if in a fist. He gripped her arms, felt her leaning toward him, her body fluid, her lips wet and glistening.

Suddenly she pulled back, looked around, cleared her throat. "I, uh . . . Good night." She spun around and half ran off.

For a moment, Cord thought about following her. But he didn't. She'd make up her own mind about what she wanted. Or didn't want.

He got his room from a friendly clerk who talked

the entire time, managing to cover the weather, the shoot-out in the saloon, the Civil War and the outrageous price of beds, all within the two minutes it took to register Diamondback and, for a two-bit tip, tell him Duncan Toth's room number.

As he climbed the stairs Cord realized for the first time how tired he felt. His legs were heavy, heavier with each step. His arm slid wearily along the banister.

The best that could be said about the room was that it was clean and had a bed. The sheets weren't fresh, but Cord didn't mind. He quickly stripped off his clothing, climbed beneath the quilt, his .45 tucked snugly under his pillow.

Sleep was instant, surrounding him like a warm lake. He sank deeper and deeper.

Until hard metal pounded on thick wood.

He swam for the surface, legs kicking, air bubbles streaming out of his nose. He heard the loud pounding again just as he broke surface.

Cord rolled out of bed, the .45 clutched in his right hand. "Who is it?"

"Killer . . . help . . . Lilith . . . dead . . ." the voice gasped, continuing to hammer at the door.

Cord quickly slipped into his shirt and pants. Standing off to the side, he unlocked the door and pulled it open.

Danny DuBoir stumbled into the room, pointing a shotgun in Cord's face. "Abracadabra," he said, clicking back the hammers.

12

"Killer . . ."

"Just a second, son."

"Fire . . . blood . . ."

"Easy now with that thing."

"Silas . . . Lilith . . ."

"Talk to me, boy. Something happen to your sister?"

"Abracadabra . . ." Danny staggered forward into the room, the twin twenty-eight-inch barrels of the Remington ten-gauge wavering as he tried to keep his balance. He was panting heavily, practically choking each breath down. Not out of hatred as before, but exhaustion. And fear.

Diamondback moved slowly, his eyes fixed on the shotgun. Both hammers were cocked and Danny's sweating fingers stayed too close to the trigger to try anything sudden. Cord tossed his own gun onto the bed.

"Easy, Danny." Diamondback held up both hands as he moved toward the lamp. "I'm just going to light this so we can talk better. Okay?"

Danny coughed, gasped in a lungful of air. "You don't understand. Silas. Scarf."

Diamondback struck the match and touched it to the wick, tilting the glass bell over the flame. The room swam with a dim light. When he turned back to Danny, he flinched at what he saw.

The young boy's face was cut all over where it had been lashed by branches. There was a large swollen bruise on his forehead where he'd fallen. His hands were skinned and bleeding. A three-inch gash oozed blood along his cheekbone. Unmistakable bullet wound.

"What happened, Danny?"

The boy sagged wearily against the wall, using the shotgun as a cane. His breathing was still shallow, but he was starting to bring it under control. "Horse shot. Had to run."

"All right now, just relax." Diamondback started toward him. "We're going to take you over to Dr. Goldhaven and let him take care of that wound."

Danny shook his head violently, hefting the shotgun back into firing position. "They're out there. Kill me. Abracadabra."

"What are you talking about, Danny? What do you mean, 'abracadabra'?"

"Abracadabra!" he shouted hysterically. "Hocus-pocus. Killers!"

Diamondback could see the boy was in shock. His body was shivering, sweat was dripping into his eyes, and he kept smacking his lips as if his mouth were dry. And now he was waving that shotgun around as if determined to use it.

Diamondback took a step toward him. Everything had to be easy, gentle. One barrel of that shotgun would send hundreds of metal pellets ripping through his body with enough force to tear his head off his neck.

As he moved toward Danny Cord flashed back to earlier that day when he'd moved toward Danny's brother. He saw himself back at the tree, the barbed wire sizzling his hand, the hot flames snapping at them, the desperate cries for help. He'd failed to help Silas, just as years ago he'd once failed to save his own brother. He wouldn't fail again.

"Just come with me, Danny. We'll go to Dr. Goldhaven's."

"*No!*"

"You can bring your gun."

"They're out there. They'll kill me. They'll kill the whole family."

The boy was terrified of going out and Diamondback didn't think he'd be able to convince him otherwise. He looked into Danny's frightened eyes and saw Lilith's smooth features reflected. On her those features were stunningly beautiful, but on her brothers they seemed too delicate, too fragile.

"Okay, Danny. How about you stay here and I'll go bring Dr. Goldhaven back? They won't see you that way."

Danny bit his lower lip, just as his sister had done earlier, and considered this idea. He wiped the sweat from his face with his sleeve. "I don't know . . ."

"You can keep your shotgun."

"I don't know."

There was a sudden shattering of glass.

A heavy thump.

Sizzling.

Danny yelled at the sound, swung his shotgun toward Cord.

Diamondback spun around, saw the jagged shards of window. Watched the brown stick of dynamite roll toward the bed, its short fuse hissing with sparks.

There was no time for considerations of which was more dangerous—Danny, hysterical with fear pointing his shotgun, or the thick stick of dynamite only seconds from detonating. There was no time for thinking. Only moving.

Diamondback sprinted toward Danny, taking advantage of the distraction the dynamite caused to shoulder the shotgun aside. One of the barrels went off, blowing out the rest of the window before Cord managed to wrench it away from Danny and toss it onto the bed. Without hesitating, he wrapped an arm around the boy's waist and snatched him off his feet, running for the open door with as much speed as he could.

They were not quite through the door when the dynamite exploded.

13

He was flying.

As if a great gust of enchanted wind had plucked him from the mortal ground and lifted him into the heavens to soar with hawks. Except it wasn't the heavens. It was the Deerlodge Hotel. And there weren't any birds. Just Danny, limp and bleeding under his arm. And he wasn't flying. He was being thrown.

And the enchanted wind was dynamite.

Cord felt the shower of splinters behind them, most glancing harmlessly off their clothes, a few stabbing into them like tiny daggers. The loud explosion echoed in his ears long after it was over. He was propelled down the hall with a powerful velocity, his body twisting so that he thought for a moment he was falling from a high cliff, dropping downward instead of horizontally. Finally he slammed into a room door. Room 247. The brass "7" dug into his chin and peeled a chunk of flesh off. The door buckled and cracked down the middle. Screams pierced the broken door and were joined by shouts and hollering from all over the hotel.

Cord bounced down the corridor a few more feet before stopping. He lifted his sore head, saw he still had Danny tucked under his arm.

"Come on, Danny. Come on." He dragged himself to a sitting position and leaned Danny against the wall. Danny's eyes were half-open slits, glazed and far away. He was muttering to himself.

A couple of half-naked men came charging out of their rooms to investigate.

"Holy Christ!" one cowboy said, whistling and shaking his head.

Dark clouds of smoke and dust tumbled out of Cord's room. The doorway was now twice as wide as it had been. The brass bedframe was halfway into the hall. Feathers from the pillows swirled amid the smoke.

A cowboy scratched his head with his pistol and wrinkled his nose at the mess. The only thing he was wearing was his gunbelt. "What the hell happened?" he asked.

Cord shrugged. "I was smoking in bed."

The naked cowboy nodded. "Dangerous habit. Me, I chew." And with that he went back into his room and closed the door.

A portly man in a long nightshirt rushed down the hall. "You all right, mister?"

Cord nodded, struggling shakily to his feet.

"That boy don't look so good."

Another cowboy volunteered to fetch Dr. Goldhaven and ran off still wearing his long-johns.

The chatty clerk who'd registered Cord a few hours earlier trotted down the hall moaning. "Oh no. No. Mr. Webster will be furious. I'm only the clerk. This sort of thing really isn't my responsibility. I hope Mr. Webster understands that."

Cord hooked the clerk's arm as he ran by and swung him around. "Better check the room for fire. I had a lamp going. Some of that smoke might be a fire."

The clerk's face collapsed in panic. "Oh no! Mr. Webster will kill me. He expects me to work miracles. I'm practically alone here."

Cord increased the pressure of his fingers on the clerk's arm. The clerk winced and shut up. "Start a fire line. I don't see any flames, but it's best to be safe."

"Yes, fire line. Good idea."

"Now give me the master key to the rooms."

"But I don't see—"

"We have to evacuate. Just in case."

The clerk hesitated. Cord pressed harder.

"Yes, of course. Evacuate." He reached into his pocket, handed Cord a key.

The portly man in the nightshirt was peering into the smoky room. "Don't see no flames," he called back, coughing. "But smoke's pretty thick. Can't be sure."

"Fire line!" the clerk shouted. "Fire line!"

Several men scrambled to form a bucket brigade, passing down buckets of sand that were stacked at the end of the hall.

Diamondback quietly lifted Danny up and carried him down the stairs, setting him on the divan in the lobby. The boy rolled his head several times, mouthed something silently, then whispered, "Abracadabra."

Townspeople were running toward the hotel,

some carrying buckets of water. In the distance a fire bell clanged steadily. Among those running toward the hotel were Dr. Goldhaven and the cowboy who'd gone to get him.

Diamondback left Danny, searched behind the clerk's desk, found an old Smith & Wesson and took off down the hall of the first-floor rooms. Most of the doors were open, with people hauling their bags and goods out as quickly as possible. But the one door Cord was looking for was closed.

He dropped to one knee, worked the master key into the lock and pushed the door open. It swung with a long whine. He dove into the room, rolled once, then sprang to his feet with his gun aimed at the bed.

But the bed was empty.

Duncan Toth was gone.

14

"So, it's started."

"It's started," Cord said, leaning over Dr. Goldhaven's shoulder as the old man tended to Danny's wounds. "How bad is he?"

"Bad enough. Multiple lacerations to the face. Bullet wound on his cheek. According to how you described him, he was already in deep shock before the damned explosion. Now . . ." He let the rest of the sentence hang uncertainly. He swabbed the furrow on Danny's cheek with alcohol and shook his head. "Tell me, Christopher, is this the typical way you proceed when trying to peacefully settle a dispute."

Cord's jaw tightened. "I didn't throw the dynamite, Professor. Don't blame the target."

"Still, you came here, announcing so grandly to everyone how you were going to solve all their problems. For a small fee."

"Not such a small fee."

Dr. Goldhaven waved a hand in annoyance. "That's not the point."

Danny stirred, his eyes still closed. "Abracadabra," he gasped. "Hocus-pocus. Silas."

"What the devil . . . what's he talking about, Christopher?"

"I don't know. He mumbled the same thing before the explosion."

"Hmmm. Delirious." Dr. Goldhaven continued cleaning the wounds. "As I was saying, the point is that you've made things worse. You and your friend, what's-his-name."

"Toth."

"Yes, Mr. Toth."

"He's not my friend."

"Well, he should be. You're the same kind, you two."

"No, we're not, Professor. You should know better."

"Should I? Perhaps. I am old, and maybe I don't see things as clearly as I once did. But I can see that someone tried to kill you."

"It happens. Sometimes people don't want an argument settled. Especially if they think they may not get what they want."

"But this time a young boy was almost killed in your place."

Cord frowned. "Someone went to work on him before he reached me. It sounded as if he were trying to warn his sister. Seemed to think someone was trying to wipe out his entire family."

The voice came from behind them. "And who might that be?" It was Tina Jennings, her long hair tangled from sleep, her blouse missing a button where she'd tried to dress too quickly. "Did he say who was after him?"

Judgement at Poisoned Well

"Not really," Cord said. "Just vague phrases, apparently unrelated."

"Like what?"

Dr. Goldhaven turned to face her. Despite the hour and the abrupt awakening, he was as immaculately groomed as he had been earlier. "He repeats his sister's name. And Gena Scarf's. Mr. Diamondback's been mentioned a few times."

"That doesn't tell us much." Tina sighed.

"Nor does 'abracadabra' and 'hocus-pocus.' "

"What?"

"He's said both words several times."

"What's he mean?"

Dr. Goldhaven shrugged. "I can't even guess. Perhaps he saw a traveling magic show once. They're quite popular out here."

She walked over to the wooden table and looked down at Danny who was sleeping fitfully. "Looks like a bullet wound."

"It is," Diamondback said.

"Any ideas as to who shot at him?"

"None."

"Any ideas as to who tossed the dynamite into your hotel room?"

"None."

She stared silently into his eyes. Neither wavered.

"You seem to be the center of a lot of activity in this town, Mr. Diamondback."

"I've always been very popular." He nodded. "Even as a child."

"Where's Duncan Toth?"

"I don't know. Did you check his room?"

"Yes. He's gone."

"Maybe the hotel was too noisy for him."

"Damn it, Diamondback," she shouted, "this isn't a joke. That boy's been chased and shot and someone tried to blow you up. A lot of people could've been killed."

"Tina, Tina." Dr. Goldhaven waved a hand to silence her. "Not so loud. Danny needs to rest."

"I'm sorry, Doc." She sighed again. "But . . . hell, I don't know what to do next."

"We can start," Diamondback suggested, "by eliminating those who couldn't have done it."

"Fine. But who can we eliminate?"

"Gena Scarf and her man Grodin. Both are out of town hunting up hired guns."

"But they could've sent one of their men from the ranch to do it," Dr. Goldhaven said.

Cord shook his head. "No. They wouldn't have known I was here."

"That doesn't mean that her men aren't responsible for chasing Danny," Tina said. "Especially after what happened to Silas. Maybe some of her men just let things get out of hand."

"Maybe," Cord said. "I've seen that kind of blood lust happen before."

"And there's still Duncan Toth."

A fist banged insistently on the front door.

"Now what?" Dr. Goldhaven grumbled, smoothing back his white hair. Tina and Cord watched him cross the living room and unlock the door.

"Good evening, Dr. Goldhaven," Gena Scarf said. "Mind if I come in?"

"Of course I mind, Gena," he growled. "But that hasn't stopped anybody so far tonight."

Gena Scarf stepped into the room, followed by

Judgement at Poisoned Well

the ever-present Jim Grodin. The bruise on Grodin's jaw had lost some of its color.

"Evening, Tina. Or should I call you Sheriff?"

"Sheriff," Grodin snorted. "Shit."

"Shut up, Jim," Mrs. Scarf snapped, and Grodin clenched his teeth. "Sorry about him, Tina. The size of his brain isn't in proportion to the size of his body."

"It doesn't matter," Tina said.

Gena Scarf lifted her eyes into Diamondback's face. They were as arctic-blue as ever. She brushed back the white lock of hair from her forehead. "Did you decide to take my offer after all, Mr. Diamondback?"

"Not exactly."

"Then what are you doing in Poisoned Well? You don't expect to work for the Providence Valley ranchers?"

"Not exactly."

"Then what exactly are you doing here?"

"That can wait, Mrs. Scarf," Tina broke in. "Right now, I've got to ask some questions about what happened tonight."

"Yes, we just rode into town, but we heard all about the fuss over at the hotel. What's happened?"

Tina Jennings explained everything, including what had happened to Silas DuBoir. And Danny DuBoir. And the dynamite.

"And you think I might have had something to do with all this?" She sounded more amused than angry.

"It's possible."

Grodin shook his huge head. "We was on the trail the whole time. We wasn't even around here.

Hell, we just rode into town a couple minutes ago."

"Now, now, Jim." Mrs. Scarf smiled. "We can't expect them to take our word for that. Can we, Sheriff?"

Tina ignored the question. "Nobody's accusing anybody of anything. Just yet."

"That's good, Tina." She grinned icily. "Because your husband's job is not a sinecure."

"But for now, Mrs. Scarf, Dave is the sheriff. And I'm the acting sheriff." Tina smiled back, though Cord could see the nervousness beneath the smile as she faced one of the state's most powerful women.

"For now." Mrs. Scarf nodded.

The discussion was interrupted by the loud clomping of horses galloping down the street. The horses stopped outside as angry voices shouted to each other. Diamondback recognized two of the voices.

Lilith and Joseph.

There were some hasty questions addressed to the townspeople still standing around, a few shouted answers, the last one being, "Over at Dr. Goldhaven's."

Within seconds they barged through the front door, first Joseph and another bearded man, then Lilith followed by the rest of the men. When they say Gena Scarf and Jim Grodin, they swung their shotguns into position.

"Hold it now," Tina said, waving her hands. "Put those things down."

"We'll put them down," Joseph snarled, "as soon as you lock those two up."

Grodin stepped in front of Gena Scarf, dropped his hand to his gun, but was wise enough not to draw it out.

"It's all right, Jim," Mrs. Scarf said, stepping out from behind Grodin. "I'm perfectly safe."

Lilith DuBoir walked stiffly past them toward the back room. "Danny. How's Danny?"

Dr. Goldhaven rested a hand on her shoulder. "He should be fine. The wounds are superficial. Right now it's the deep shock we have to be concerned with. I've given him something to help him sleep."

"Oh, God, Dr. Goldhaven," she gasped, her hands trembling at her mouth. "He looks so pale."

"He'll be fine. Just give him some time."

"But his face, there. That looks like a bullet wound."

Dr. Goldhaven nodded.

Lilith spun around to face Diamondback, her eyes wide and glaring. "He's just a child, I know he came after you, but did you have to shoot him?"

"He didn't shoot him," Tina explained.

"He must have! On the ride back to Providence Valley, Danny broke away from us and grabbed one of the shotguns. He screamed that he was going to kill you, Mr. Diamondback, for not saving Silas. He was pretty shaken, unwilling to listen to reason." She wrung her hands together as if to keep them from shaking. "We tried to track him down, but he gave us the slip pretty easily in the dark. Finally we decided to ride back to town to warn you. That's when we found out he was hurt in the explosion."

"Someone tried to kill Diamondback," Tina said. "Danny was in the room with him when the dynamite was thrown."

"But the bullet wound on his face?"

Diamondback padded to the sofa, still barefoot, and perched on the arm of the sofa. "Danny was chased and shot by someone before he reached town. By the time he got to see me, he was muttering deliriously."

"What did he say?"

Cord looked around the room, studying each person in turn, trying to fit the pieces together as he spoke. But he couldn't. Not yet. "Sounded like a warning for you. As if he thought you were next. I don't know. And something about 'abracadabra' and 'hocus-pocus.'"

She frowned with confusion. "What does that mean?"

"I don't know. But he's repeated it a couple times."

She shook her head. "Maybe something he's read in a book. I can't explain it."

"He also mentioned you, Mrs. Scarf."

"I told you!" Joseph shouted. "I told you she was behind it." He hefted his shotgun.

"I had nothing to do with this," Gena Scarf said calmly.

"Then your men did. You gave the orders."

"When I do give the orders to hunt you people down," she replied with a thin smile, "I won't deny it. I'll take credit for it."

Diamondback stood up, walked slowly to the center of the room, his thumbs hooked on the corners of his pockets. All eyes followed him.

"The way things are going, it's just possible that you're all going to get exactly what you deserve. Which is probably a sudden bullet and a shallow grave. However, we can prevent all that with some simple negotiation. You both have strong points on your sides, but if you try to fight it out, what's happened today will keep happening. Again and again."

"That's just fine with me." Grodin grinned.

Diamondback turned to him. "Glad to see the swelling's going down, Grodin. You don't look as silly now."

Grodin started angrily toward Diamondback, but Gena Scarf laid a restraining hand on his arm.

Cord smiled. "But tomorrow it can happen to anyone. A bullet out of nowhere. A knife. A stick of dynamite through your window." He looked at Mrs. Scarf. "Tied to a tree with barbed wire, then burned alive."

"I didn't—"

He cut her off. "However, we could work out this whole thing fairly so that everyone can live with the situation."

"How?" Lilith asked.

"By hiring *him*, that's how." Mrs. Scarf laughed. "Right, Diamondback?"

"Right. The ranchers of Providence Valley have already agreed to listen to my suggestions tomorrow night. All you have to do is let me come out to the Rocking S and tell you exactly what I'll tell them. If it doesn't make any sense, you can always go back to killing and butchering each other. I'll gladly be on my way."

"We don't need no advice from you," Grodin said. "Mrs. Scarf's been handlin' things okay."

Diamondback leveled his dark eyes on Mrs. Scarf's blue ice chips. "What have you got to lose?"

She stared back unflinchingly for almost a minute before nodding her head. "Okay," she said, marching toward the door with Grodin in tow. "Tomorrow evening at the Rocking S. I'll listen. But that's all." She shoved aside two of Lilith's burly friends and walked out the door.

"A waste of time," Joseph grumbled to the others. "We can't trust her, and we can't trust him." He pointed at Diamondback.

"We've already given our word to listen," Lilith explained patiently. "And we shall keep our word. Anything to prevent more bloodshed. Doctor, we'd like to take Danny back with us now."

Dr. Goldhaven shook his head. "I'm sorry, Lilith, but he can't be moved just yet. He may have internal injuries that haven't shown up. I'll have to keep him here another day or so, just to be safe."

She considered this, biting the edge of her lip as she thought. "Okay, Dr. Goldhaven. We thank you for your help." She nodded at Joseph and he quickly opened the door. "Good evening," she said to the three of them and hurried through the door, her friends trotting after her. Joseph tossed one final menacing glance at Cord before slamming the door shut.

"Well," Tina said to Cord, "I guess it's up to you now. I hope you're as convincing tomorrow night as you were tonight."

"He'd better be," Dr. Goldhaven said with an accusing tone.

A groan came from the treatment room.

The three of them went back to find Danny struggling in his sleep, his head whipping back and forth, sweat shaking onto the floor.

"Abracadabra," he moaned. "Hocus-pocus."

15

"You scared?"

"Yes."

"How come?"

"I'm always scared."

"I don't believe you." Tina Jennings laughed nervously, shifting around on her horse for the hundredth time. She tilted her head toward Diamondback, her black eyes glinting a spark of moonlight. "Besides, aside from somebody tossing dynamite at you, you've got nothing to be afraid of."

"And you do?"

"Damn right I do." She sighed deeply. "You wouldn't understand. You're big and strong, obviously got a real education, clever. And white. Me, I'm a Chinese woman whose father fills bathtubs and whose husband is a professional target for drunken cowboys and desperate criminals. That's enough right there to keep me scared every hour of every day."

They rode silently in the dark for a few more minutes, following a wagon road toward Mrs. Scarf's Rocking S Ranch.

"What scares you, Cord? I mean, really."

Diamondback laughed. "Everything. Really."

She shook her head in the dark. The moonlight washed silver threads through her black hair. "The way you handled yourself after the explosion. The way you handled both Gena Scarf and Lilith's group. I don't know. I've been terrified ever since Dave rode out of here and left me with his badge. I can't believe I argued so much to wear it." She choked out another soft laugh. It sounded like rustling arbutus leaves. "You don't look like you've ever been scared."

"I've had my share."

"You're just humoring me. What have you got to fear?"

"Like I said, everything. The world conspires daily to end our lives, most of the time by means we can't prevent no matter how careful we are. A pothole in the road can trip my horse, send me suddenly tumbling to the ground. I land just the wrong way and I'm dead, or paralyzed. You stop at a farmhouse and drink a cup of milk from a cow that's been nibbling rayless goldenrod. You're dead a few days later of milking sickness. So, yeah, I'm scared of everything. Tornadoes. Floods. The three riders following us—"

Tina bolted up in her horse. "What?"

"Two over there behind the trees." He pointed. "And one up there riding point. They've been with us for the past few miles."

"Gena's men. We crossed onto her land a few miles back."

"Let's pick up the pace a little," Cord said and

Judgement at Poisoned Well

gigged his appaloosa. They took off at an easy canter, their horses clopping in the still night.

Diamondback had slept much of the day, struggling in and out of sleep, wrestling his pillow into early afternoon. Afterward he'd attacked a breakfast that would have fed three ordinary men. Then he'd checked in on Dr. Goldhaven and Danny. Danny was still resting quietly, occasionally mumbling inaudibly. Dr. Goldhaven was administering medicine and strong advice to several patients. Always the teacher, he lectured each on the virtues of either safety, cleanliness or moderation, depending upon their complaint. He had thawed some toward Cord, but he was still upset at the effect of Cord's arrival on his little town.

"I didn't cause any of this, Professor," Cord had explained. "Don't kill the messenger just because you don't like the news."

"Chaos." Dr. Goldhaven had spat the word out like a curse. "Soon it will be every man for himself again. No law, Christopher. Only chaos."

Diamondback hadn't argued the point. He'd seen it happen before, in bigger towns, to more civilized citizens.

"Over there." Tina pointed.

Several buildings loomed up in the distance, their outlines glowing in the bright moonlight. Barn, stables, bunkhouses, the main ranch house. Big. Impressive.

They finished their ride in silence.

The front door opened as they were dismounting. Jim Grodin stood in the doorway, his huge body blocking any light from leaking out of the house.

"Let's go," he said, jerking a thumb.

Diamondback and Tina followed him into the house. Inside, it was even more impressive than outside. The furnishings were not elaborate, but they were tasteful. And expensive. A large fire crackled in the stone fireplace.

Mrs. Scarf was posed next the mantel in a light cotton dress. The fire behind her revealed every curve and dimple under the cloth. It was obvious she wore no undergarments. But even without the staged effects, she was an attractive sexy woman. Cord remembered their thrashing in his tub and smiled to himself.

Gena Scarf patted back her white lock of hair, staring only at Cord, ignoring Tina. "Well, I promised you your say. Now say it and get lost."

"Well, at least you have an open mind. I can't ask for more than that."

"Don't patronize me, Diamondback. I only agreed to hear your little sales pitch out of, well, pity for the kid. Danny."

"Maybe out of guilt?"

She stood, legs apart, hands planted on her hips. The fire behind her outlined the silhouette of each shapely leg. "I'm not guilty of anything. Except protecting what's mine."

"The ranchers of Providence Valley have rights too," Tina said. "After all, they own the land."

"Sure, now. Now that we've fought off the Indians. Chased down the rustlers. Took the sting out of the land. Now they come in and the government sells them what wasn't theirs to sell in the first place."

Diamondback wandered to the left as he spoke, placing the wingback chair between himself and

Judgement at Poisoned Well

Grodin's nervous gun hand. "Why didn't you just buy the land?"

Gena Scarf choked out a bitter laugh. "With what?" She waved her hand around the room. "This ranch costs money to run. We meet all our bills and usually have some left over. But we had a couple bad years, lost some cattle during the winter. Hell, I couldn't afford to buy any new land. I was swimming upstream just to keep hold of what I already had."

"And now you're willing to lose it all in a war with these ranchers?"

She shook her head. "You don't understand. Drifters like you never had anything of your own to fight for. Maybe that's why it's so easy for you to hire out your guns. But my husband and his daddy built the Rocking S. Lost a lot of their family doing it. Died younger than was fair. Now these Holy Roller–types come in and string barbed wire across the ranges. How am I supposed to feed my cattle? Without those ranges half of my stock will starve. You don't expect me to just sit here and let that happen?"

"There are ways," Cord said quietly. "Compromises that can—"

"I don't want to hear any of that. I don't have to compromise. I've got enough men to make others do the compromising."

Tina took a few steps toward Gena. "It don't matter how many men you got, Mrs. Scarf. You got no right to harm those people. Dave will be back in town in a couple days, and as the sheriff—"

"That's in a couple days, Tina." Gena Scarf smiled.

Tina's voice was hard and flat. There was none of her previous nervousness in it. "If I find you've had anything to do with what happened to Silas and Danny, you'll hang. I swear it."

Gena Scarf's smile froze onto her lips. "Jim, show these people out."

"One more thing, Mrs. Scarf," Diamondback said. "I'd like to talk to Toth."

"So? Why ask me?"

"Because he's here."

She stared at him, blue eyes tipped with ice. "What makes you think he's here?"

"Because I know Duncan Toth. If you want to find him, look for the money."

A minute of silence, then a door at the back of the room opened.

Duncan Toth, sketch pad in one hand, cup of tea in the other, entered with a grin. "My own blend," he said, raising his cup slightly. "The secret's in the cinnamon."

"Mr. Toth," Tina announced, "I have a few questions for you."

"I'm sure." He nodded, setting the tea on the table and dropping onto the leather sofa. He propped the sketch pad on his knee, began drawing. "I suppose it's about that business at the hotel last night."

"We missed you," Cord said.

"Apparently someone missed you too."

"Where were you at the time of the explosion?" Tina interrupted.

"Right here. Waiting to discuss business with Mrs. Scarf. I like to get the financial details settled early." The fire cast a flickering shadow across his lean face, bringing out the more sinister edge to his features. With his smooth words and outrageous style, it was sometimes easy to forget how dangerous this man could be. But Cord wouldn't forget. In Missouri he'd seen Toth slit a rustler's belly with a Bowie knife, then reach in and yank out the intestines, holding it up for the dying man to see.

"That's right," Gena Scarf said. "He was here."

"How do you know?" Cord said. "You were just riding into town at the time."

"He was here when Grodin and myself got here. Several of my men confirmed he'd been here waiting for me."

"Not much of an alibi."

"But enough." Toth smiled. "Right, Sheriff?"

Tina frowned. "For now. Where can I find you when I need to?"

He sipped his tea, appraised Gena Scarf with a sly smile. "Right here at the Rocking S."

"*In town*," Gena Scarf said firmly, as if it were a discussion they'd had before. "At the hotel."

Toth shrugged. "It was worth a try." He glanced up at Diamondback, grinned, continued sketching. "Don't give me that sour look, Diamondback. I know I'm disgusting, that's why people hire me more than you. I'm corrupt and therefore corruptible. They understand that. But your righteousness makes them nervous. Nobody likes to hire someone they suspect is better than they are. Puts them at a moral disadvantage."

Diamondback smiled. He recalled using similar phrases in describing Lilith DuBoir and her group from Providence Valley.

Mrs. Scarf gestured with her chin. "Jim."

Grodin stepped forward. "Let's go you two. Out."

Tina stood firm. "Just a word of warning to both of you. So far the town's remained neutral in this fight. But even they have a limit. They're already pretty stirred up about what happened to Silas and Danny DuBoir. And now the dynamite in the hotel. That threatens their lives as well as their livelihood. They're starting to blame you, Mrs. Scarf. And with the town backing the Providence Valley ranchers, you can't win this fight. I wouldn't do anything else to anger them."

"The hell with them." Gena Scarf sneered. "I'll do whatever I have to."

"Tough lady," Toth said, sketching away.

Grodin reached out his huge hand and shoved Cord forward. "I told you to move it."

Toth chuckled. "I wouldn't do that."

Grodin snapped around. "Shut up, Toth." He turned back to Diamondback, shoved him again even harder. "I said move it, you stupid sonofab—"

Diamondback grabbed the thick hand under his arm, pulling Grodin forward. Surprised, the big man stumbled toward Cord. Diamondback swung his elbow back in a wide arc, smashing the bony point into Grodin's mouth. Two front teeth exploded out between mashed pulpy lips, bounced across the wooden floor like tumbling dice. Grodin grabbed his swollen mouth, saw the blood seeping through his fingers.

"Thun of a bith," he lisped through the gap in his teeth. He spun on Cord, his hand dropping toward his gun.

Judgement at Poisoned Well

"Count your blessings, Grodin," Toth said quietly.

Grodin hesitated, looked at Gena Scarf. She looked away, something like pity on her face. Grodin stomped out of the room and out the front door.

Toth stood up, shaking his head and chuckling. "You can see why she needs me, Diamondback. Nothing but big, dumb shitkickers out here." He walked toward them, his sketch pad hanging at his side. "Oh, look at this. A drop of blood on your Navaho rug." He ground it in with the toe of his boot. "Hardly see it now." He smiled at Mrs. Scarf, then at Diamondback. He lifted the sketch handed it to Cord. "A little present."

Tina leaned over and stared at the paper, a slight gasp in her throat.

It was as beautiful as the last one, the details sharp and penetrating, but with a spirit and power that transcended the image. It was a drawing of Diamondback. At least it was the same shape of the body, the same clothes he'd worn the day before. But it was hard to tell for sure, since the body was lying facedown. His Shofield .45 was clutched in his right hand. A wisp of smoke curled from the barrel. A gaping hole of shredded flesh and shirt in the middle of his back. Blood soaking through the shirt. But there were no trees, no plants, no buildings, nothing to indicate where the body was. And the shading made it impossible to judge whether it was night or day.

"Nice," Cord said. "Better than a lot of those illustrations I've seen in the dime books."

"Really?" Toth looked genuinely pleased.

"Sure. Easily as good as James Walker."

"You think so?" Toth cocked his head, studied the drawing again. "Maybe you're right."

"Stop it!" Tina finally shouted, a slight touch of Chinese accent creeping into her voice. "I don't know which of you is crazier. But I know you can't go around threatening to kill people in this town, Mr. Toth. I heard what happened at the saloon last night, and I'm still not convinced about your whereabouts when the dynamite went off."

Gena Scarf held up her hands. "Listen, Sheriff—"

"Shut up!" Tina snapped. "I've about had it with you and your hired killers. I agreed to accompany Mr. Diamondback out here because I thought there might be a peaceful solution to this whole thing. But it looks like you're determined to have your own private war." She stopped herself, hearing her own Chinese accent. When she spoke again, it was slower, more controlled. Without accent. "One more incident"—she nodded at the drawing—"and I'll request federal troops from Fort Durning. And they'll tie everybody's business up so tight you'll be lucky to get any ranching done." She slapped Diamondback on the arm as she marched past him. "Let's go."

He suppressed his smile and followed her out the front door.

They were half a mile away before either spoke again.

"You were something back there," Cord said, urging his horse next to hers. "Fearless."

"Ha! Didn't you notice my little Chink accent coming back like a bad stutter?"

"No," he lied.

She looked over at him, shook her head. "Damn it, I thought maybe you'd pull it off. Make peace somehow. I know I didn't think much of the idea at first; what with you getting paid made it seem not right. But I thought, hell, if that's what it takes, okay. If anybody can do it, he can." She sighed. "Now what?"

"Now we ride over to Lilith DuBoir and explain. They're expecting us."

"Okay. Let's take the short cut." She yanked her horse around, nudged it into the woods.

Diamondback followed, heard a bubbling stream. He didn't like that. The sound drowned the other sounds he always listened for. Like hoofbeats. Twigs snapping. They hadn't been followed when they'd left the ranch, but that didn't mean they wouldn't be again.

They picked their way slowly through the trees until they came to the stream. They let their horse dip their heads for a quick drink.

Cord kept looking over his shoulder, uneasy for no particular reason.

"Do you think Duncan Toth will really try to make his drawing come true?" Tina asked.

"If he gets the chance. He thinks he owes me one."

"Why doesn't he just call you out in a fair fight?"

"Because he knows I won't accept."

She looked surprised. "Why not?"

"Because he's faster."

"But—"

The shot exploded, severed a branch behind

them. Tina cried out, was knocked out of her saddle into the stream.

Another shot cracked the night.

Cord dove into the shallow stream, banging his elbows and knees on the rocks. He glanced over at Tina who was facedown in the water. Blood swirled and floated, suspended in the water like black ink.

A third shot.

A loud plop in the water a few feet from Cord. The horse whinied, galloped off through the trees.

He scrambled through the cold water, scooped Tina in his arms and splashed across the creek. Quickly he dodged behind a tree, sank to the ground, still cradling Tina.

But the shots kept coming.

16

Splinters of bark sprayed into Cord's face. He ducked back behind the tree, his gun cocked, his eyes searching the darkness for a target.

"Gun," Tina muttered behind him, stretched out on the ground.

"It's in your holster."

"Oh." She propped herself onto her elbows, touched a hand to her throbbing forehead, dabbed her fingers in thick sticky blood. She reeled groggily. "How much longer do I have to live?"

"I'm no doctor," Cord said, helping her sit up. "But I'd say another fifty, maybe sixty years."

"Huh?"

"You were shot in the thigh. The blood on your head's from where you hit yourself when you fell. It knocked you out for a few minutes."

She looked down at her left thigh, saw the dark streak where the bullet had raked out the flesh. Now she felt the stinging pain. "It hurts," she said simply, her head still fuzzy.

Another shot boomed through the woods. The

bullet rustled leaves before smacking into the tree trunk, kicking up a spray of splinters.

"He's over there." Cord pointed to where he'd seen the gun flashes. "Looks like he was waiting for us."

Tina pulled her gun out of her holster, waved it weakly. "Want me to cover you?"

He looked back at her with a shocked grin. "What for? He's got a rifle. A Winchester .44–.40 I'd say. All we have are pistols. He's on horseback and our horses have run away."

Tina looked frantically around. "My buckskin?"

"That's right. Besides, you aren't in any shape to cover me with a blanket, let alone a gun. And I'm not anxious to go running through the dark woods with the moon at my back."

"So what do we do?"

"We get him to come to us."

"How?"

"We wait. If we lay low and don't shoot back, he won't know whether or not he's hit us. He'll have to check it out."

"It's Toth, isn't it?" she said angrily. "He's making good on his drawing. He had enough time to saddle up and follow us."

"Maybe. Or maybe Grodin. He lost face tonight for the second time in front of his boss. That can make a man do about anything. Now lay back."

She flattened herself on the ground, her gun clutched across her stomach.

"Let me take a look at that wound." Cord hunched over her leg a moment, then clicked open his folding knife. Careful not to make any noise, he sliced the pants open around the wound.

"Not bad," he whispered. "It's already stopped bleeding. But it'll leave a sexy little scar."

"Great," she whispered back. "I need all the help I can get."

They waited in silence for twenty minutes. There had been no more shots, no other sounds but what was natural to the woods. The stream boiled nearby. An owl screeched, then fluttered away. The night breeze whooshed through, ruffling trees like a parent mussing a little boy's hair. Nothing.

Then something.

Cord lifted his head, cocking an ear. A faint crunch of boots on dry leaves. Nothing more. He nudged Tina, who had drifted off to sleep. She opened her eyes, started to say something. Cord clamped his hand over her mouth and shook his head. She nodded understanding.

They lay still, their guns ready. Listening.

A branch rustled. A twig snapped.

Cord had positioned their bodies so that only his unmoving leg was visible. And Tina's blood-smeared hand. Enough to distract his attention. Meanwhile they both lay side by side, their guns ready.

Another twig. He was closer.

Then an owl bolted from its nearby branch, screeching a complaint. The ambusher spooked and fired at the bird. Tina, thinking he was firing at her, rolled out from behind the tree and began shooting back. It was too soon, Cord knew, but rolled out too, his gun spitting fire and bullets.

One of their bullets hit him. He hollered, fell backward, scrambled to his feet and stumbled off into the woods, dragging his rifle behind him.

"Let's get after him," Tina said, scurrying up. She took one step and pitched forward. "Owww. My leg!"

Cord quickly dragged her back behind the tree, just as a rifle shot cracked and a bullet thudded with a splash of dirt next to her head.

"He still has the rifle," Cord reminded her.

It was several minutes before they heard his horse riding off a full gallop.

"Did you see who it was?" she asked.

"No, too dark. You?"

She shook her head. "But I still think it was Toth. And when we get out of here—"

"We're not going anywhere for a while."

"What do you mean?"

"I mean that we have no horses, and you can't walk on that leg, and I can't carry you back to town. We're spending the night right here."

"You could make it back to the Rocking S, then come back for me. That's only a few miles."

"What if our ambusher is from the Rocking S? Grodin, or Toth, or one of the others she hired?"

She flipped her wet hair behind her shoulder. "I see what you mean."

"So we stay, get some rest. By morning you should be able to hobble along with some help."

"I don't suppose we can chance a fire?"

"Nope. Too risky."

"I figured." She sighed. "It's just that it's getting cold."

"We'll have to improvise," Cord said. He stood up, found a dead tree stump and cut a large hunk of bark out. Then he kneeled next to Tina and began shoveling a long trench with the bark. Half an hour later he had a shallow bed dug, just wide enough for the two of them to squeeze together.

"Pretty smart," she said as he helped ease her down. "But it reminds me a little too much of a grave."

"Well, it gets worse, because once we're in, I cover us both with a layer of dirt to keep in the body heat."

"Oh, Christ."

"Crude, but effective." He climbed in next to her, started brushing dirt over them.

She stopped his hand. "Could we wait a little before we do that? Give me a chance to get used to the idea of lying here first."

"Sure."

She took a deep breath of relief, swallowed hard, shifted uncomfortably. "You knew someone was out there, didn't you? I mean, before, when we were watering the horses."

"Not really. Just had a feeling."

She nodded. "I could tell. My grandfather could do stuff like that. And more. Hear people talking before anyone else could, through solid walls sometimes. Describe things without even looking. Spooky guy." She turned onto her side facing Cord, her head propped on her hand. "My father said grandfather lost a lot of those abilities when he came to this country. Every year he could do less and less."

"What happened to him?"

She shrugged. "Disappeared. Worked on the railroad for a while with my father. They both sent money to their families in San Francisco. Me, my mother, my grandmother. We lived with two other families. Then one day my father showed up alone. Never talked about what happened to grandfather. And the funny thing is, I was the only one who ever asked. It was as if my mother and grandmother already knew without asking. Or maybe it didn't matter how it happened. I don't know. But here we are, twenty years later. My father fills tubs and I play sheriff."

"Were you born in China?"

"San Francisco. I'm first generation. I didn't learn English until I was five or six and didn't use it regularly till much later, which is why I still struggle with an accent sometimes. What about you?"

"Nothing to tell."

"Oh, mysterious stranger, huh?"

He laughed. "Something like that."

"What a pair. We fit right in at Poisoned Well. A town originally called Garden City, founded by prospectors searching for some legendary gold mine the Indians always talked about. Well, damned if someone didn't find a big strike one day. But he was so afraid that everybody else in the town would jump his claim, he sneaked down one night and poisoned the town's only well. Killed almost two hundred people before they strung him up. Then when they examined his 'rich' claim, it turned out to be nothing more than pyrite. Fool's gold. Some history, huh?"

"Pretty much like most of the towns out here."

"That's the sad truth."

He turned onto his side, faced her. "What about you?"

"Me?" He could see her skin flush, even in the pale moonlight. "Nothing to tell."

"Come on. That's my line."

"Well, I met Dave Jennings when he was just elected sheriff. He came to Timberline to help the old sheriff there on a posse. We met at the hotel where I worked with my father. We fell in love. He was crazy enough to marry me, despite his friends' advice. Marrying someone Chinese is only slightly better than marrying an Indian, though both fall below murdering small children and cannibalism on the social-acceptability scale."

Cord laughed again. Then she laughed too. Then, without either knowing how it happened, they were kissing. Tenderly at first, tongues playfully sliding past teeth, probing wetly. And then passionately. Arms hugging, bodies pressed and grinding.

Mindful of her wounded thigh, he started to pull away. But she sucked his tongue into her mouth and rubbed her breasts against the hard muscles of his chest.

They began tugging at each other's clothing. Cord eased her pants over her narrow hips. "Better keep our shirts on against the cold." Cord said.

She nodded absently as she unfastened his pants. Underwear and pants were piled into pillows. Cord placed one under her head, the other under her buttocks.

Still concerned about her injury, Cord started to ask if she was all right. She quickly mashed her lips against his, drowning his words.

"Don't speak," she said. "Please. If you do I might chicken out. And I don't want to chicken out."

He saw that she was shivering slightly and wrapped her tightly in his powerful arms. They kissed again, rubbing their naked bodies against each other, building a heat that burned away the evening chill.

Cord's rough bandaged hands slid gently over her breasts, small soft mounds with long dark nipples. She wriggled against his hand for more pressure. Teasingly, he brushed his fingertips across the nipples until they budded up toward the moon. Then he stroked her skin down along the rib cage, feeling each bone beneath the taut skin, over the protruding hipbone, sloping down into the course pubic hairs.

He let his fingers rake through the straight thick hairs, so unlike the curly hairs of white women. He slipped his middle finger over the rim, dipping lightly into her wet vagina. The tender folds of flesh were slick with oily juices as he slid his finger slowly in, to the first knuckle, the second. All the way. She gave a little hop with her hips as she spread her legs, moaning for more.

He eased another finger into her, then another finger, stirring gently as she rotated her hips and grabbed his neck.

Cord opened his eyes and saw her staring at him, a smile on her lips. Sweat had beaded along her forehead and nose. Her angled eyes fluttered as he plunged all three fingers as deep as they would go.

She reached down, folding her hand around his, pulling his hand out of her and up to her lips. His sopping fingers glistened in the moonlight. With a sly smile she licked each finger, sucked it until her juices were gone. Cord felt a hot tingle spreading across his stomach as he watched, felt his penis twitch anxiously. Then Tina reached down with her finger, touched the tip of his penis, and brought her finger back to her lips. Cord could see his own sticky juice like a drop of white honey before she licked it off her finger.

He climbed onto her, careful about her thigh, but with an urgency commanded by both their desires. She arched her back, guiding his thick penis into her body, finally swallowing it with a deep gasp.

Diamondback moved slowly at first, with a mounting rhythm Tina matched. He felt the cool sweat from their bodies pooling against their stomachs, splashing each time he thrust forward. The shirts scratched at times, but with the moon this bright he couldn't chance her seeing the scars on his back. Discovering who he really was. Even in sex he could never totally abandon himself. Never give all the way.

"Cord," she moaned, her eyes closed, her mouth open, panting. Then she said something in Chinese.

Her hands reached around and grabbed his bare buttocks, the fingers pressed against tight muscles as she urged him faster. He obliged.

"All of it," she panted. "I want all of it!"

Her finger slid down the crevice of his buttocks, pressed against his anus. He bucked against her faster now, rocking in their dirt bed like two fighting animals. She moaned in short bursts, pushing herself against him as she pulled him closer. Then her movements became sharp, sporadic, and she jerked repeatedly, a thin scream escaping through clenched teeth. At that moment Diamondback arched forward, and came with long writhing thrusts.

They lay there together awhile, until their sweat began to evaporate in the cool night air. Quickly they dressed, hugged each other close.

"How's the thigh?"

"Okay," she said. "All of me's okay."

"Me too."

They held each other silently.

"Cord?"

"Yes?"

"I love my husband. I just wanted you to know."

"He's a lucky man," Cord said sincerely.

"I've never done anything like this before. I mean, with anyone other than him." She couldn't bring herself to speak his name. "This has nothing to do with how I feel about him."

"I know. Go to sleep."

Her voice was angry. "Don't you feel any guilt? Ever?"

"When I deserve it. Certainly not over something as pleasurable as what we just did. If anything I should feel envy. Your husband will have you for the rest of your lives."

She buried her nose against his chest. "Thanks for that. I'm sorry."

"Good night."

The silence lasted longer this time. Thick clouds veiled the moon. The stream bubbled endlessly behind them.

"Cord?"

"What?"

"What will you do now?"

"Leave town. I have no clients, therefore no reason to stay."

"What if I got the town to hire you? I could speak to the mayor about that."

He shook his head. There was an edge to his voice. "I'm not a hired gun."

"Don't you even want to know who shot at us tonight?"

"Not particularly. When I leave Poisoned Well, whoever it is won't have any reason to shoot at me anymore."

"Unless it's Duncan Toth."

"In that case, he and I will settle up somewhere else. When we're both getting paid. In our line of work we're bound to meet again."

She lifted her head to look at him. "I don't understand you. What do you want out of life?"

He didn't answer.

"Well, answer me?" Her slight Chinese accent was back. "At least Duncan Toth knows what he wants. Money."

"I guess that puts him one up on me."

She stared into his dark eyes. "Damn you," she whispered and pulled him on top of her. She began tugging at his clothes.

17

"Half dead. I'd say."

Tina shaded her eyes and looked up at the woman in the wagon. "Pardon?"

"I said you two look half dead."

"Half dead and back from hell," the man next to her agreed.

"Simon!" she scolded sternly. "Susie is in the back."

"Half dead and back from hell," young Susie Perkins sang from the back of the buckboard, still wearing the same blue sunbonnet she'd had on the day before.

Diamondback and Tina had been walking toward town since the sun had first peeked over the horizon. They'd followed the main road, but stayed out of sight just in case their ambusher showed up again. Cord had found a branch sturdy enough to serve as a walking stick for Tina. But even so she'd only been able to move slowly. Occasionally, Cord carried her for short distances.

The Perkins family were the first travelers to come by and Diamondback had quickly swept Tina up in his arms and raced to the road to wave them down.

"What happened to you, child?" Mrs. Perkins had asked Tina, scowling at the dirty clothes and the tear in her pants that by now revealed plenty of smooth thigh around the wound. Mr. Perkins noticed too and licked his lips thoughtfully.

"We were bushwhacked, Mrs. Perkins," Tina said. "Our horses spooked and we had to sleep in the woods. We'd appreciate a ride to town."

"Certainly, child," Mrs. Perkins said, though Tina was only a few years younger. "Just climb right in the back there with Susie. Plenty of room. On our way to church. Reverend Demmings conducts the best Sunday services I ever seen." Mrs. Perkins prattled on as Diamondback eased Tina into the wagon.

"It's the bounty hunter, Ma," Susie said. "The one I tole you about."

Mr. and Mrs. Perkins turned around and stared at Diamondback. Mr. Perkins looked nervous. Mrs. Perkins looked haughty.

"It's all right," Tina said, wincing from the pain in her leg. "He's been helping me. Kind of a deputy."

"I didn't think you'd be able to appoint deputies, Tina," Mrs. Perkins said sourly, turning away from them. "Especially since you ain't the real sheriff."

Mr. Perkins looked at Tina, shrugged an apology. Tina winked at him and smiled. He snapped the reins and the wagon rattled down the road.

"Got any idea who it was that shot you?" Simon Perkins asked.

"A few," Tina said. "Nothing definite."

Judgement at Poisoned Well

"You're as closemouthed as your husband. But it don't take no medicine man to figure you was out talking to Gena Scarf. And we heard all about you, too, Mr. Diamondback. Whole town's been talking."

"And what have they been saying?" Cord asked.

"That Gena went and hired this shootist, Duncan Toth. Man with a mean reputation. Heard what he done to Scarf's boys in the saloon. Fast bastard."

"Simon!" his wife said.

He ignored her. "Now me and the missus ain't nothing but farmers. So's a lot of folks around here. We ain't a threat to either the Rocking S or the Providence Valley ranchers, but this is our home, too. And we're not anxious to have a shooting war around here, not with our kids and wives around. And I know most of the folks in town feel the same way." He paused, snapped the reins again. The horse picked up the pace a bit. Mrs. Perkins held on to her seat with one hand, her hat with the other. "I also know that, though we may not care much for those stiffnecks from Providence Valley—"

"Self-righteous, that's what they are," Mrs. Perkins interrupted. "Too good to worship in our church we built with our own hands. A mail order church we ordered from Lyman Bridges, Chicago, Illinois. Number forty in their catalog. Five thousand dollars cash."

Mr. Perkins continued as if there had been no interruption. "We may not care that much for them, but they stick to themselves and don't cause no one harm. Besides, they got the law on their side in this matter. Now, Gena Scarf spends a lot of money in this county, but that ain't gonna do us any good if we lose our families. What happened to those DuBoir boys is just plain inhuman. And we don't want it happenin' to our kin. That's why a lot of the town is already plenty riled. Enough so as to ride out to the Rocking S and tear the place apart."

"Well, Simon, you just let me handle it for right now," Tina said.

"No offense, Tina. You're about the damnedest woman I know around here. Hell, I seen you outshoot Dave a dozen times. But it takes more than shooting to be a sheriff."

"So, I've heard."

"Truth be told, I'm not sure even Dave could handle things now."

"What's your suggestion, Simon?"

"That you get up a citizens' committee, kinda like deputies."

"Vigilantes," Tina said angrily.

He shrugged without looking back at her. "Don't matter what you call it. But you're gonna need the help."

"Not that kind of help I won't."

"You may get it whether you want it or not."

Tina started to speak again, but Cord touched her arm and shook her head as if to say, "Save your strength." She nodded thanks, squeezed his hand.

Little Susie Perkins took the break in conversation to mean she could talk. She peeked out from under her sunbonnet at Cord, studying his body and face with fascination. "You gonna kill somebody today, Mr. Bounty Hunter?"

"Susie!" her mother yelled.

"I was just askin'. That's what Tommy Kohler said. Bounty hunters got to kill somebody everyday. Just to keep in practice. Are you gonna kill somebody today?"

"Depends," Cord said.

"On what?"

"On whether I get a nap. Sometimes if I don't get a nap I get real mean and kill somebody."

"You take naps too?"

He nodded. "Got to if I want to stay alive."

"Gosh," she said.

"Don't pester the man," Mr. Perkins said gently but firmly and Susie fell silent.

They arrived in town less than an hour later.

"Appreciate it if you'd take us over to Dr. Goldhaven's," Diamondback said. "I'd like him to take a look at the sheriff's leg."

"It's not that bad," Tina protested. "I can walk."

"I'll take you by," Mr. Perkins said.

They passed dozens of people on their way to church, most of whom gaped openmouthed at Tina and Diamondback, both streaked with dirt.

"Hey, Stanley," Tina hollered, cupping her hands around her mouth.

Cord recognized the chatty clerk from the hotel.

He looked frightened at having his name spoken so loudly, as if he were being accused of something.

"Stanley, did Duncan Toth come back to the hotel last night?"

Stanley stopped, tugged his earlobe nervously,

looking over his shoulder as if he expected Toth to be standing there. "Yes. He came back quite late. Came in, went right to his room." Then he scurried off toward the mail-order church.

"Thanks," she said, but he was already gone.

"He's my first stop," she told Cord.

"After Dr. Goldhaven."

She started to argue, then shrugged. "All right. But afterwards I'm going to see Toth. Where will you be?"

"Buying another horse so I can leave town."

"Then I'll go alone."

The buckboard squeeled to a halt in front of Dr. Goldhaven's white picket fence. The weedless garden rose neatly in the sun.

Cord reached up to help Tina out, but she angrily brushed him away, climbing out alone. "I don't want to keep you in town any longer than necessary."

She thanked the Perkinses and waited until they'd continued down the road before swinging open Dr. Goldhaven's gate. They could still hear the chatter of Mrs. Perkins' harsh voice as the wagon rounded the corner.

"I can handle things from here," she said to Cord.

"I'm just going in to say good-bye to Dr. Goldhaven. Have him take a look at my hands."

"Fine!" she snapped and pounded on the front door.

There was no answer.

"Come on, Doc," she said. "It's Tina."

No answer.

She pounded again. "I'm not in the mood to play, Dr. Goldhaven. Open up."

Silence.

"Sometimes he just acts like an infant." She twisted the doorknob and pushed open the door. Cord followed. There was no one in the living room. She limped ahead of him through the back door into his treatment room. "How many times do we have to—" Then she screamed a loud warbling cry that sent Diamondback vaulting through the door.

When he entered the room, Tina was on her knees, vomiting on the floor.

Then he saw it too.

And felt the rage boil within.

18

"Do something!"

Diamondback staggered forward, his knees suddenly very weak.

"For God's sake, do something!" she sobbed again.

But there was nothing to do.

It was too late.

Dr. Felix Goldhaven, the fussy old genius who had taught law to Cord's father, brother and Cord himself, was against the wall, a foot off the ground. The only things that kept him from falling were the thick rusty railroad spikes driven through his palms and wrists. They had started with the palms, but when the fragile bones and old flesh had started to tear, unable to hold the weight, they hammered two more spikes into the wrists.

But they had not stopped there.

Atop the professor's neatly combed white hair, sat a crudely fashioned crown. Of barbed wire. Scutt's Arrow Plate, a popular brand. It had been jammed onto his head with enough force to dig into his scalp and forehead, sending tiny trickles of blood like melting red wax down his face.

His glassy gray eyes stared at Cord. Through Cord. Lifeless.

The spikes had caused him great pain, but the scalpel sticking like a cold steel arrow from his chest had killed him. And the crumpled ball of soggy paper stuffed in his mouth had prevented him from crying out.

Cord rushed over, grabbed the professor by the waist and lifted him gently, as if this would relieve the pain from the spikes. Holding the professor with one arm, he yanked the scalpel out of the chest and threw it across the room. It bounced off the wall and clanged across the wooden floor. He reached up and pried the wad of paper from his teacher's mouth. The jaw had already stiffened as rigor mortis set in. A man in this much agony deserves to cry out, Cord thought angrily, shoving the paper into his pocket.

Then Tina was there, helping Cord lift the professor. Cord let her bear the weight while he climbed onto a chair and tried to yank the spikes out of the wall. He managed to pull the two from the hands, but those through the wrists were lodged too deeply into the wall studs.

"Damn Toth to hell!" Tina cried, the tears dripping from her eyes and nose as she struggled to hold Dr. Goldhaven up. "You can ride out of town now, Cord Diamondback! No one around here's going to pay for your time, but I'm going to see that Gena Scarf and your friend Toth hang for this. You hear me, Diamondback?"

Cord stepped down from the chair It was no

use. The spikes wouldn't come out. And they couldn't stand here all day holding the professor. He was dead. His pain was over. But for those who'd done this, the pain hadn't even started yet. It would, though, Cord swore silently through clenched teeth. It would.

He tried to pull Tina away, but she brushed him off, her arms still wrapped around the old man's waist, using what little strength she had left leaning on her good leg to hold him up.

"Come on, Tina," he said softly. "He's dead. No point in killing yourself."

Reluctantly she loosened her fingers and he helped her as she limped over to chair and collapsed, burying her head in her hands, her shoulders trembling with each sob.

"I'm going over to the blacksmith's and get a hacksaw," he told her. "It's the only way to get him down. I'll be back soon."

She nodded without lifting her head.

Diamondback walked out of the house. The sun was bright and warm and felt especially good on his face. Somehow it didn't seem right to him that the sun should be shining on a day like this. A day in which the world lost one of its best. And he lost a friend.

He saw a few people across the street heading toward the doctor's house with puzzled expressions on their faces. Then he saw Simon Perkins and family pulling up in their buckboard.

"Heard some screams a minute ago," Perkins said, handing the reins to his wife and hopping off the wagon. "Anything wrong?"

Had it only been a minute ago that Tina had

screamed? It seemed like hours, days. Something in his distant past. Cord hooked a thumb over his shoulder. "Inside," he said.

Several people now were rushing into the doctor's house, probably tracking in mud, messing his floor, rumpling his sofa. A lifetime of neatness destroyed in minutes.

And then he thought of something.

"Danny! Where's Danny?"

He ran back inside. People were gasping and moaning and making threats. Cord pushed past them to the back of the house, searching every room. But Danny was gone.

"Danny," he said to Tina over the shoulders of the men crowded around her, demanding action.

"Now, Tina, damn it," Simon Perkins said, "we been damned patient, but it's time you let the men do the men's jobs."

"Simon's right," another man said. "We gotta do something now."

Tina ignored them, shoving her way through the crowd men who continued to talk among themselves, fighting their fear, building their courage.

"Where is he?" she asked.

Cord shrugged. "Gone."

"My God. After what's happened here and to his brother, I hate to think what these animals are capable of doing to him. Maybe these men are right. Maybe I should let the citizens committee help me." It was a question.

Cord didn't respond. "I'll get that hacksaw now." He knew that once a bunch of vigilantes got together, things always ended the same way.

Lynching. Sometimes they got the right people, sometimes not, sometimes a combination of the two. It didn't really matter to them. It was something they did out of fear, and just taking action, whether it was right or wrong, helped kill that fear a little.

As he headed for the front door again something in the living room caught his eye. No, not something. The lack of something. He glanced over at the floor-to-ceiling shelves of books and noticed a black gap where a thick tome was missing. He looked around the living room, but saw no books lying around. Mentally he retraced his recent search of the house, didn't remember any stray volumes. He rubbed his stubbled chin, slid his hands into his pockets. His fingertips pressed against the soggy wad of paper he'd plucked from the professor's mouth. Slowly, carefully, he unraveled it, occasionally pulling too hard and tearing a corner. He didn't know what to expect, if anything. But maybe . . .

The ink was faded, washed out from the professor's saliva. But Diamondback could still make out the faded words.

Abracadabra. Hocus-pocus.

Written over and over again in Dr. Goldhaven's handwriting. Just doodles of the words Danny had muttered in his delirium. Phony incantations by stage magicians. Nothing more.

But what about the missing book?

Cord smiled. Back at Harvard the students had always poked fun at Professor Goldhaven's rumored habit of grading student papers while in the water closet. Some hinted that particularly poor papers were used improperly then disposed of. Even Professor Goldhaven was aware of the rumors and sometimes joked that he was going home to big meal of fresh fruit before grading papers. That always got a nervous laugh.

Cord was remembering the professor fondly as he rushed through the house again, out the back door and down the stone path to the outhouse. Prettily painted a bright yellow. Immaculately clean.

It was inside on a specially built bookshelf that Cord found the book, open on the shelf, a wooden tongue depressor marking the page. The book was in French. Cord began reading, occasionally skipping words he couldn't translate. He read the marked passage, leafing ahead a few pages, then back a few pages. Finally he closed the book.

And understood.

19

On his way to the blacksmith's, Diamondback made one stop, careful not to be seen by anyone. It took only five minutes, then he hurried down the street, and explained to the smithy why he needed the hacksaw. The blacksmith was a short barrel-chested man with burn scars all along his thick arms. But as soon as Cord told him what had happened to Dr. Goldhaven, the man tore off his leather apron, grabbed the saw and ran down the street, waving for Cord to follow.

Word had somehow traveled all the way back to the church, because people were pouring out of the high double doors and racing toward the doctor's house.

By the time Cord got back, there were townspeople cluttered all around the house, leaning against the white picket fence, standing in the neat little garden. Some of the women were crying openly while their children played tag in the street. Men shouted angrily, slamming their fists into open palms as they made speeches and threats.

People stepped aside as Diamondback neared them, opening a path to the door.

Inside, things were worse. Simon Perkins was still there, surrounded by prosperous-looking men in expensive suits. The local merchants.

"We've lost the only doctor in the whole damn county," Perkins said to the crowd of men. "And he was only helping out until we got a replacement for Dr. Flannery. How long we been lookin' for a replacement now? Six months?"

"More like eight," one of the merchants corrected.

"Eight months! What're we gonna do now when our children get sick? Or our wives? Lay down and die?"

"No!" a few men grumbled.

"And who might be next? The sheriff when he gets back? The schoolmistress? You? Me?"

More grumbled protests.

Cord worked his way through the tight crowd of men and saw Tina in the back of the treatment room. Someone had found a hacksaw and had already sawn through the spikes. Tina and a couple men were lifting Dr. Goldhaven onto the wooden treatment table.

"Got a mob on your hands," he told her.

"Maybe they're right," she snapped, looking into the professor's lifeless eyes.

Cord reached over and closed the lids. The mouth was still open from when he'd pried out the paper. The professor looked like he was trying to say something.

"Tina!" Simon Perkins said. "Are you going to deputize us or not?" It was a command.

Judgement at Poisoned Well

"I don't need no deputies, Simon," she said. "When I do I'll let you know."

"What do you intend to do about this? Two murders and a kidnapping!"

"I intend to investigate."

"Investigate!" he said incredulously to the crowd. "Hell, woman, it's too late for any damned investigation. It's time for action!"

The crowd roared its approval. A few pistols were brandished.

"I say the citizens committe goes on over to the Deerlodge Hotel and grabs ahold of that Duncan Toth fella. And we shake him until we get some answers. Stanley Dowd said Toth was still there."

"Yeah," the men shouted. "Let's go."

"Now, you men stop," Tina said. "I'm sheriff until Dave gets back and—"

"Sorry, Tina," one of the merchants in the expensive suits said. "But we don't see how Dave had the right to make his wife actin' sheriff. As a member of the town council, I have to question his authority."

"Damn right!" Simon said. "C'mon men!"

The men plowed through the house, squeezing out the front door in a mass of churning anger. Cord heard a lamp crash, a table tip over.

Tina took a deep breath. "I better go along and see they don't get into trouble. They're basically decent folks."

"They'll hang him," Cord said.

"Toth?"

"That's right."

"I doubt it. But so what if they did? I figure he probably has it comin'."

"Probably."

She gave him a look. "What's that supposed to mean?"

He pulled out his gun, checked the loads. There were a few scratches on the barrel from the explosion in his hotel room, but it worked fine. He slipped it back into the holster. "Be seeing you."

"Where you going?"

"The livery stable. I have a horse to buy."

"Leaving town after all, huh?" she said scornfully. "Your 'decent folks' are waiting."

She stormed past him, pushing him aside, though he wasn't in her way. "Bastard."

"Probably."

The horse wasn't as good as the Appaloosa, but the price was right and it looked like it could ride hard without too much problem. He was a Morgan, fifteen hands high, with a dark brown coat. He wasn't as young as Diamondback would have liked, but the breed was intelligent, hardy and good-natured. More than enough for what he had in mind.

"Got a good saddle?" he'd asked the livery owner, Abel Drew.

Drew had frowned, pursed his lips and scratched his butt before answering. "New or used?"

"Used."

"Got a couple over here. Take your pick." Abel Drew wasn't more than forty, but he was almost totally bald. There were always a few large stable flies buzzing around the top of his head. "Got your Texas saddle here." He pointed. "A couple of Denver saddles. This old mission saddle I can let go cheap." He swatted at the flies over his head. "Or this California saddle. Ten pounds lighter than the Denver saddle. Real pretty leather tooling too. Looks good and keeps you from slipping. Almost new." He started laughing a dry hacking laugh. "Some cowboy rode in here one day, got hisself drunk as an Indian, shot up the saloon. Dave Jennings threw him into jail for a week. By the time he comes out he owes me a week's care and feedin' of his horse. Well, naturally he didn't have enough to pay for it. Had to sell me his saddle. Rode out of here bareback and mad as hell." He snickered, waved the flies away.

"I'll take it." Cord smiled. "At the same price you paid for it."

"But I gotta make a profit, mister."

"You did. When you bought it off that cowboy for half of what it was worth. I know you didn't make a deal like that without bragging around town about it, so I'll check out the price before I ride out. If I find you've overcharged me, well . . ." Cord shrugged sadly.

"I ain't gonna cheat you," Drew said, swallowing hard.

"Diamondback!" Tina's voice echoed through the stable.

"Over here, Sheriff," Drew hollered quickly, relieved at the company.

"Hi, Mr. Drew." Tina nodded as Drew scuttled off to saddle Cord's horse.

"How's the citizens committe? Which tree is Toth hanging from. I'd like to catch a glimpse on my way out of town."

"Toth wasn't there. The clerk said he'd been

there all morning, but when Simon and the rest of them broke into his room he was gone. The window was open."

"Now what?"

"Well, the committee is pretty brave when it comes to cornering one man in a hotel room, but they aren't anxious to ride out to the Rocking S. Not with Gena Scarf and her pack of guns. They're over at the saloon trying to decide what to do next."

"What would you have done if Toth had been there?"

She stared into his dark eyes. "I wouldn't have let them lynch him. I'd like to see him hang for what he's done. But not like that. You've gotta believe me."

He nodded. "I do. Now what?"

"Now I'm riding out to Providence Valley. With Toth gone and Danny missing, I think it might be a good idea to warn Lilith. Get some of the ranchers to band together so they aren't picked off one at a time."

"Good idea. You'll make a good sheriff after all."

She smiled. "Nope. Once this is over I'm turning my badge back to Dave. If he ever lets me talk him into something like this again, I'll . . ." She shook her head. "I don't know what."

"All set, mister," Drew said from a distance, the Morgan saddled, bridled and pawing the ground.

"Well." Tina sighed. "I guess this is it. So long."

"So long." He paid Drew, climbed up onto the Morgan.

Tina hesitated, started to say something but then just turned her back and started to walk away.

Cord called after her, "Who's riding out to Providence Valley with you?"

She stopped turned to face him. "No one."

"Could you use some company?"

She fought the smile spreading across her face. "Sure, if it's not out of your way."

"It's not."

They passed the barbed-wire fences that stretched through the valley. Many had been cut, the wooden posts burned or knocked down.

"Scarf's men," Tina explained. "The valley ranchers started complaining about it months ago. Dave did what he could, warned Gena Scarf, but it didn't help. And he couldn't be out here watching their fences all day and night. So the ranchers started posting their own guards. Shot a couple of Rocking S hands, killed one of 'em."

"And then the Rocking S had to retaliate and so forth."

"That's right. But no one figured it would ever get this bad. Not really."

"They should've figured," Cord said. "It's happening all over. Over in Missouri, I saw a cow gutted and a rancher who'd been stringing barbed wire stuffed into the dead cow's stomach and sewed in it—still alive."

She made a face. "That's disgusting."

"It gets worse."

"There," she pointed, leaning forward in her

saddle. "Right over that ridge is the DuBoir ranch. We're almost there."

Cord nudged the Morgan and it took off over the ridge and down the other side, responding quickly to each tug of the reins. Tina's quarter horse finally caught up as they pulled up in front of the ranch house.

"That's odd," Tina said, glancing around as she climbed out of the saddle. "There's nobody around."

"It's Sunday. Maybe they're at that church they built."

"The church is back there in the woods, just a quarter mile through those trees."

Diamondback brushed the dirt from his clothes. "At least we washed and changed before leaving town. I don't want to embarrass you, what with reelection coming up and all."

She laughed, knocked on the front door. "Lilith?"

Cord stood back from the door and waited. It was a small ranch house, half the size of Gena Scarf's, but it had a homey, efficient look from the outside.

Tina knocked again. "Lilith? It's Tina Jennings."

The door opened and Lilith stood in the doorway. She was wearing a white cotton gown and smiling. Her strawberry-blond hair hung straight to her shoulders. She looked even younger, to Cord, and even more beautiful. "Hello, Sheriff," she said, her smile widening to include more of her perfect teeth. "Hello, Mr. Diamondback."

"Hi." Cord nodded.

"Can we come in, Lilith," Tina said. "I want to talk to you."

Lilith's face went blank. "It's not Danny is it? He's all right, isn't he?"

"Let's talk about it inside, okay?"

Lilith stepped back numbly to admit Tina and Cord. The room was clean but sparsely furnished, mostly with crude handmade furnishings.

"What about Danny?" Lilith asked, wringing her pale hands.

Tina explained. Painfully she described Dr. Goldhaven.

"My God," Lilith gasped. "That's blasphemous. Sacrilege." She sank slowly to the chair next to the fireplace. "But what about Danny? Where's Danny?"

"I don't know," Tina said quietly. "But we'll look for him. The whole town's angry and anxious to bring this damn thing to a stop."

"But will they stop Gena Scarf and her hired killers?"

"Yes. If they could have found Duncan Toth this morning, they would have tried to hang him. I think they'll definitely help you people now."

"Good," Lilith said, staring off absently. "Good. It hasn't been easy for my people you know. We've been persecuted for hundreds, even thousands of years. They burned seven thousand of us at Treves. Five hundred at Geneva. Eight hundred in Würzburg, fifteen hundred at Bamberg. History has not been kind to our cult. Now, for once, people will help us get what we want."

"Cult?" Tina asked. "What are you people exactly? Quakers? Jews?"

"Not exactly." She grinned, her eyes focusing sharply on Tina and Cord.

The door to the kitchen was flung open and two

bearded men burst through with shotguns leveled at Diamondback and Tina.

"I don't understand, Lilith," Tina said, her face confused.

"Don't you, Sheriff?" Lilith said, her grin wicked with contempt. "Then let me explain. We are Satanists."

"What?"

"Devil worshipers," Diamondback said, raising his hands.

20

The heavy trapdoor slammed shut behind them, echoing through the cavern with a tomblike finality. The dirt ceiling and walls were reinforced with strong timber, but the floor was still dirt. Lilith lifted the hem of her white robe and led them down the passageway. Lanterns hung from each wooden post.

"Where are you taking us?" Tina asked.

"Patience, dear Sheriff."

"What are you going to do with us?"

Lilith giggled. "Something special."

The two husky men prodded Tina and Diamondback with their shotguns, urging them to walk faster. Cord no longer had his .45, folding knife or the derringer he usually stashed in his boot. The search had been brusque but thorough, with a shotgun pressed at the back of his head. They had searched Tina just as roughly, though lingering a bit when feeling her breasts and crotch. Lilith had watched and giggled.

Afterward they had been lead through the pasture behind the ranch house, into the woods, until

they came to the massive church built in a clearing.
The church had stained-glass windows and an ornate
cross poking straight into the sky. The inside
had row after row of wooden benches, all empty,
facing a raised altar. Behind the altar was a life-sized
statue of Christ on the cross, painstakingly
hand-carved from teak. Even the veins in the
arms were clear.

One of the bearded men propped his shotgun
against the wall and, grasping the head of statue,
twisted it sharply. The head swiveled until it faced
the opposite direction and a trapdoor in the altar
floor slid open.

"It's much bigger down here than up there,"
Lilith explained. "We have many tunnels and rooms
down here, as well as a grand meeting hall.
Naturally, we had to keep up certain appearances,
just in case. Hence the ridiculous church above
us." She sighed. "A small price, I suppose, for
safety."

They rounded another corner, walked down a
long flight of dirt steps and into a huge room,
almost twice as large as the church above them.
There were wooden benches here too, with long
narrow tables that also faced an altar. Atop the
tables in front of the people were heavy brass
goblets. A statue of Christ similar to the one in
the church above rose behind the altar, but with
several grotesque differences. This statue was upside
down. And sitting on the now-top of the
cross, was a great laughing demon, horned with
cloven feet and a serpent's tongue. The carving
was cruder than that of the Christ, but more impressive
in its raw angular power.

Seated at the long wooden benches were several of the men Cord had seen in town accompanying Lilith. They sat with their families, wives on one side, children on the other, all dressed in white cotton robes, though some were smudged with dirt, or gray from too many washings. They all had the gaunt, stern expressions of the devout.

"Mr. Garrison." Tina pointed. "Mrs. Garrison. What are you doing here? What . . . ?" She trailed off, shaking her head with shock. "Dave saved your son from drowning last year."

"Did we forget to thank you?" Mrs. Garrison grinned.

"But there's Bill Forrest, the Timmonsons . . ."

"Everybody in Providence Valley is here, Sheriff," Lilith explained. "We are all one family. That was the plan from the beginning. To find a place where we could all move together. To send out an open invitation to all our brethren. Then to build our own empire."

Diamondback chuckled. "You may have Providence Valley, but that's—if you'll pardon the expression—a hell of a ways from an empire."

Lilith clapped her hands together and laughed, her blue eyes twinkling with delight. "Oh, Mr. Diamondback. Providence Valley is only a small beginning. There's so much more land around here."

"But that's Rocking S land." Tina said. "Gena Scarf's."

She wagged a finger at Tina. "Not for long."

"I don't understand."

"Let me try to explain," Diamondback said. "These people all come out here from other places, mostly New England. They buy as much land as they can. But the big parcels, the real choice lots belong to the Rocking S. Well, to get that land they have to get rid of the Rocking S."

"Very good, Mr. Diamondback." Lilith nodded.

"But how?" Tina asked.

"Fortunately, the Rocking S needed Providence Valley for grazing. These people could have worked out a leasing deal with the Rocking S, but instead they wanted to force them to a fight. One Gena Scarf couldn't win legally. But that wouldn't have been enough. They may have hurt the Rocking S, but it would still exist, and still own the same amount of land. So they started by weakening the structure. How did Mr. Scarf die?"

"Fever." Tina shrugged. "Doctor never could figure it out."

"How soon after his death did that doctor return to the East?"

"A couple months."

"I figure the farthest east he got was a six-foot hole in these woods. Right, Miss DuBoir?"

Lilith continued to smile, but there was a hardening around the lips and eyes. "Go ahead, Mr. Diamondback. You're telling it."

"Mr. Scarf was probably poisoned. The doctor eventually figured it out."

"But why didn't he tell us?"

"I don't know. Fear or greed, probably both."

"Mostly greed," Lilith said disgustedly. "He figured it out that we poisoned him, all right. Confronted Joseph and a few of the others. Told everyone else that Henry Scarf died of fever. Then turned around and bled us every month."

"Until you finally got rid of him."

She smiled. "He had it all written down in his safe, but we got that, too. We just made it look like he'd sent for all his stuff, loaded it up, brought it out here, and Mr. Timmonson there cracked it open like a soft-boiled egg."

"Now that Henry Scarf was gone you thought it would be easier to work on his wife. But she was tougher than you figured."

"We thought she'd jump at the chance to sell and take her money to some fancy big city. But she didn't."

"That meant you needed one more thing to beat her. Support from the town. And now you've got it."

Tina shook her head as if dazed. "No, Cord, that doesn't make sense. Silas' was wrapped in barbed wire and burned alive. And Danny—"

Diamondback's face was grim, his teeth clenched.

Lilith looked solemn for a moment, then she was smiling again. "Unfortunate, of course, but sacrifices are sometimes necessary for the good of the whole."

"My God," Tina gasped. "You killed them. Your own brothers?"

She looked pleased at Tina's horrified reaction. "Naturally. We needed to get the townspeople to back us. It was the only way we could drive Gena Scarf out. As His priestess, it was my decision to select someone. I selected Silas."

"And Danny didn't know?" Diamondback asked.

"No, I thought it best not to tell him until later, when he understood the situation better. But then after he went crazy and attacked you, I decided to tell him the truth. But he only became more enraged, grabbed a shotgun and rode away. Joseph and some others rode after him, tried to kill him, but he got away. They managed to track him into town, saw him enter the hotel where you were staying, apparently to tell you everything."

"So the dynamite wasn't meant for Cord, it was meant to kill Danny!" Tina said.

"Unfortunate, but necessary. However, again Joseph's incompetence allowed Danny to live. But it proved to be another opportunity to turn the town against Gena Scarf."

"You killed your two brothers and Dr. Goldhaven for that!" Tina yelled. "Just to get the town angry at Mrs. Scarf."

"The land is worth hundreds of thousands of dollars, Tina," Diamondback explained. "Eventually millions."

"And even more important," Lilith said, "we will have a place where all of us can live freely, without persecution."

"And rich."

She smiled slyly. "With Satan's help."

"You're sick," Tina said, her accent clipping the edge of her words. "All of you are sick!"

"What do you know?" Lilith hissed. "We have survived for thousands of years despite every attempt to kill us off. We worship a stronger god."

There was muttered approval from the others.

"But you've killed your own family."

"So?" She shrugged. "I also killed my parents on the trip out here." She fingered the sash that held the robe in place. "The greatest danger to our sect is draining away through loss of our children.

So through the centuries we have approved methods of providing for all their needs. They don't ever have to go outside the group for anything. But because we are often isolated from others of our faith, parents have had to fulfill these needs."

"What are you saying?"

"Incest," Cord said. "They practice incest. Keeps the children from looking for other mates and leaving home."

"God, no," Tina said. "It's too horrible."

"My own father took me, though I had warned him I was different. I was His priestess. Not to be touched by any but those I chose. Still, he kept doing it. Mother didn't help, though I warned her too. She said it was something we just had to accept. They couldn't see that I was special."

"So you killed them?"

Lilith nodded. "Poison. Then I brought Silas and Danny out here, where Daddy had already made arrangements."

Tina stood quietly, limp and reeling as if all the life in her had been drained out. Her eyes were half closed, sleepy. Cord saw that she was in a mild state of shock and put his arm around her waist to keep her steady.

"Now what?" Tina asked, her voice distant, as if no answer could matter. "Now what happens?"

"Now"—Lilith brightened, an eager smile spreading across her pretty face—"the ceremony begins!"

1

"Some deserve to die. Others deserve worse."

Her followers murmured approval.

Lilith nodded to the crowd. A husky man in a white robe at the back stood up and walked off down a corridor.

"What are you going to do with us?" Tina asked again.

"Relax." Lilith smiled. "And learn."

The man in the white robe returned, pushing Joseph in front of him. Joseph struggled, but his hands were tied behind him. He wore nothing but a red cloth wrapped around his waist. His beard had been shaved. A bullet wound punctured his forearm.

"Ah, Joseph," Lilith said as if he were a tardy guest they'd all been expecting.

"Please, Lilith. Please," he pleaded, digging his naked heels into the dirt. The man in the robe shoved him in the back and he stumbled forward, tripping over the corner of a bench. He sprawled face-first into the dirt.

"Oh my." Lilith clucked her tongue. "Please try

to be more careful Brother Joseph. This is an important ceremony."

"Let me explain," Joseph sniveled, mucus bubbling from his nostrils. The man in the robe reached down, grabbed Joseph by the hair and yanked him to his feet. Joseph winced as he staggered up the altar steps to stand next to Lilith. The man in the white robe followed.

Lilith turned to her followers and raised her hands. "In the name of Our Father, Beelzebub, Lord of Darkness, this man Joseph Elliott stands before us accused of failure to perform his duties, thereby putting all our lives and fortunes in jeopardy. First, in the matter of Silas DuBoir, his incompetence almost caused Silas to be saved by this nonfaithful, Cord Diamondback."

"How could I know he'd be riding by?" Joseph cried, his voice little more than a rasp.

Lilith ignored him. "Second, in the matter of Danny DuBoir, he failed not only as the leader of the tracking party, but again with the dynamite."

"Please, Lilith," Joseph begged and sank to his knees with great shivering sobs.

"Cord," Tina whispered.

Diamondback squeezed her shoulder to comfort her. There was nothing else he could do. Yet.

"Third," Lilith continued, "he failed last night in the ambush of Sheriff Jennings and Mr. Diamondback, managing only a pitiful wound to the sheriff's leg. Worse, receiving a wound himself that could have led them to us."

The congregation looked at Joseph with disgust.

"With Lucifer's scaled hand guiding you, I ask for your verdict."

Judgement at Poisoned Well

Each member of the congregation, in unison, picked up the brass goblets in front of them, raised them in the air and chanted together, "We drink his blood!" Then they drank from the goblet. One little boy dribbled down his chin, spilling it on his robe. His mother reached over and smacked his hand.

"Is it really . . . really . . ." Tina hesitated.

Cord looked at the crimson stain on the little boy's gown and nodded. "It's real blood."

"Oh, Jesus!"

Lilith held her hands high again. "We give thanks to Danny DuBoir, whose sacrifice provided us with our Holy Communion of Blood." Then she turned to Joseph, her face grim with resolve, the eyes slightly mad. She nodded at the husky man in the robe. "Proceed."

Quickly he grabbed Joseph and wrestled him onto the thick wooden table on the altar platform. The table was a slab of sturdy oak more than a foot thick with short legs less than a foot long. It was situated directly under the inverted crucifix so that it looked like the carved devil was staring down at it, laughing.

Joseph's hands and feet were strapped to the legs of the table. He continued to struggle and twist and buck until the man in the white robe became impatient, grabbing him by the hair with one hand and slamming his head against the table. Joseph was slightly dazed but still conscious. Once the ankles and wrists were bound, the man yanked the red cloth from Joseph's waist. He lay spread-eagle on the table, completely naked.

"Lilith, please," he moaned. "You can stop this. You can reverse their verdict. You have the power."

Lilith walked over to him, patted his cheek with gentle strokes, and smiled benevolently, like a mother to her naughty child. "I have the power," she repeated softly. Then she untied the sash to her robe and shrugged it off her shoulders, letting it puddle around her feet.

She turned slowly, her arms raised, her body also naked.

It was one of the most magnificent bodies Diamondback had ever seen. Long pale neck melting into narrow shoulders. Firm round breast like full moons, the nipples pink, almost colorless. The waist trim, flaring slightly where hipbones protruded against taut skin. The pubic mound wispy, slightly darker than her strawberry-blond head, looking like a feathery cloud resting between her legs. The buttocks small and solid as they met the long shapely legs.

The congregation stared, the men perhaps a little more intently than the women. Occasionally a wife would glance secretly at her husband's face, but nothing was said.

Joseph, despite his predicament, was also affected by the power of her beauty, for his penis had risen from a shriveled nub to a semi-erect position.

Lilith looked down at it, her smile mischievous now, like a little girl playing a prank. She reached down, closed her hand around his penis, squeezed. Immediately it was fully erect. She let go.

There was no preliminary touching or caressing or kissing. She simply climbed atop the table, straddled Joseph's hips and slid his penis into her vagina. Joseph was no longer pleading, though his face was creased with horror and pleasure. Lilith rocked back and forth like a little girl, never changing the rhythm. But Joseph began to move faster now, straining his hips against hers, bouncing his hips off the table.

Lilith stared down at him with curiosity, as if he were a new species of insect she'd never seen before. As she rocked she lifted one hand and the man in the robe brought her a heavy brass goblet. She clutched it in one hand, raising it toward the carved demon in from of her, as if toasting him.

Joseph was moving frantically now, pumping against her, moaning and panting. "Now, Lilith," he gasped. "Please do it now!"

She rocked faster now, her breasts bouncing with each movement. A thin film of sweat trickled down her spine, disappearing in the crack of her buttocks.

Then Joseph lifted his whole body off the table, his eyes and teeth clenched as he howled, "Now, Lilith!"

Lilith hopped rapidly up and down, her buttocks slapping his thighs. Joseph trembled against her. "Yes," he rasped. "Yes, yes, yes."

And while Joseph enjoyed the final ecstasy of orgasm, Lilith lifted her goblet to the carved demon, drank her brother's blood, then smashed the heavy brass into Joseph's skull.

"Yes," he cried out and she smashed his skull again. A sickening crack echoed in the room as the skull caved in, splashing a wave of blood against her chest. She smashed him again and again, the skull collapsing in chunks, sticky blood splattered across her body, his body twitching against hers as the nerve endings fought death. Then nothing.

Lilith climbed off Joseph's still body, stood in front of the congregation, and smiled. "Thus do we do His work, for the glory of His Kingdom."

The crowd chanted approval, toasting her and draining their goblets.

"I'm going to be sick," Tina told Cord.

"No you're not!" he said. "I need you strong and tough if we're going to survive what comes next."

Lilith slipped her robe back on, the blood on her body soaking through, and turned to Tina and Diamondback. "Now, what are we going to do with you two?" Her smile widened as she pointed at Diamondback. "Strip him and strap him to the table."

The two men with shotguns stepped forward.

"You're insane!" Tina screamed.

The congregation laughed.

The two men leaned their shotguns against the table where Joseph's body lay oozing blood and brains, and grabbed Cord's arm. The husky man in the white robe took the front of Cord's shirt in his fists and ripped it open. Within seconds they would all know that Cord Diamondback was really Christopher Deacon. Not that it would matter to them. If anything it would probably make them admire him. Before killing him. But the timing was all wrong. And survival right now depended on timing.

"No speeches first?" he asked Lilith. "No sermons on the superiority of Lucifer?"

"No need. After all, we're not missionaries out to convert anybody. Besides, you're the ones about to die. But like poor bumbling Joseph, you will die at the height of pleasure. First you, then—" she turned to Tina—"you."

"No!" Tina snapped.

"Don't worry. You'll like it with me." She pivoted back toward Diamondback. "Get on with it."

The man in the white robe reached for Cord's belt buckle.

"Fire!" someone in the congregation yelled. "Fire!"

Everyone turned to where he was pointing. The passageway leading back to the church and the trapdoor was filled with thick black smoke. It drifted out lazily at first, in little curls. But soon great balls of smoke rolled into the room like giant tumbleweeds. Several of the children began coughing, crying for their parents.

Then, out from the black smoke like Lucifer himself, stepped Duncan Toth, a gun in each hand, a cocky grin on his lips. "What's this? A party and I wasn't invited. Shame, shame."

Cord shook his arms free from the two men. "If you'd have waited any longer, it would have been too late," he barked at Toth.

"It took me half an hour to figure out how to open the damned trapdoor."

"Toth!" Tina said. "How . . .?"

"Later," Cord said, pulling her off the altar toward the passageway.

Suddenly the room was an explosion of movement.

Lilith pointed at the three of them, her teeth

bared, her face almost ugly with hate as she shrieked, "Kill them! Kill them!"

Without hesitation, the congregation moved to obey. The two burly men who'd held Cord's arms dove for their shotguns just as Cord was stepping off the altar. Toth swiveled toward them, firing both guns. Both men groaned as they crumpled to the ground, dead or close to it. In the meantime, the men in the congregation were fumbling under their robes for their guns.

"Give me one of your guns!" Diamondback yelled at Toth.

"Get your own." Toth laughed as he blazed away into the congregation. Two men's robes blossomed red as they fell backward, their guns skidding across the floor.

"Kill them!" Lilith screamed. "In His name!"

Diamondback saw several guns swinging toward him. Immediately he dropped to the altar floor, tucked his shoulder and rolled toward Joseph's table. He could hear the bullets thudding into the wooden floor, following him only inches behind. Finally he bumped into the table, grabbed one of the shotguns and, holding it at waist level, popped up on the other side of the table. When he did, he was looking into the twin barrels of the other shotgun, now leveled into his face by Lilith. It was braced against her shoulder, and one of her eyes was closed, the other peering down the sight.

She giggled, her lips twisted cruelly as she started to say something.

Diamondback pulled both triggers.

Her head disintegrated into a shower of dripping goo and matted hair that flew back out over the congregation like a swarm of insects. Her headless torso stood for a moment as if confused, one finger still resting against the trigger. Then the body swooned, spiraled into a lifeless lump of spare parts.

The shooting stopped almost immediately. The congregation stared in shock at the remains of their priestess. Mothers and their children came out from under the tables, rubbing their eyes from the increasing smoke. Some of the younger ones pleaded to go to the bathroom.

Tina was crouched on one knee, pointing one of Toth's guns. Toth stood next to her, his remaining gun in his left hand, a throwing knife raised in his right hand.

Cord quickly snatched the shotgun from Lilith's hands. Her fingers opened easily, like smooth pale petals of some exotic flower. He hurried over to Toth. "What about the fire?"

"Just a diversion. Nothing but smoke and a little flame. It'll be out in a few minutes."

"All right, let's get out of here while we can."

"What about them?" Tina asked.

"We can bolt the trapdoor and keep them here until we can round up a few more deputies."

"Sounds reasonable," Toth said.

The three of them backed out into the passageway, their guns still aiming at the congregation. But no one followed them, no one shot at them. When they were around the corner of the tunnel, they turned and ran for the exit. As they were climbing up through the trapdoor they heard the low monotone chanting rumbling down the passageway behind them, "Hocus-pocus. We drink of Her blood, we eat of Her flesh!"

Tina glanced at Cord, a horrified expression on her face. "You don't think . . ."

Cord nodded.

"Jesus. Goddamn cannibals." Duncan Toth pushed his floppy hat back on his forehead and scratched his chin with his knife. "Damnedest bunch of folks I've ever seen. And those robes"—he shook his head disdainfully—"You'd think they never heard of tailoring."

Tina gaped at Toth, her mouth open with amazement. "You stupid . . ." She shook her head, tried again. "Don't you . . ." The words died in her throat and she shrugged. Suddenly she was laughing, hysterically at first, as if comprehending for the first time everything she'd just seen, everything she'd heard. As her mind tried to absorb it all, accept it, file it away, she laughed crazily, tears drenching her face. Then she cried. Diamondback held her against his chest, felt her tears against his skin.

Toth looked on, uncomfortable. "Sorry," he told her.

Tina lifted her head, wiped her eyes on Cord's shirt. Her almond-shaped eyes were slightly swollen, but the black pupils glistened. "You were right," she said to Cord as she pushed herself to her feet, favoring her wounded leg. "There's more to being a sheriff than shooting well."

22

"You lousy sonofabitch. You knew!"

"Suspected." Diamondback corrected.

Gena Scarf looked unconvinced, glaring at him as she brushed the lock of white hair from her forehead. "And you, Toth, you're supposed to working for me."

"I was. But Diamondback made me a better offer."

"What better offer?"

He grinned. "My life."

The four of them sat in the sheriff's office sipping coffee. Tina Jennings leaned back behind her husband's desk, her coffee untouched. Toth was perched on the edge of the desk, drinking his own special blend of tea, sketching on his pad. Gena Scarf sat erect in her chair, her face stony and confused. Diamondback stood by the stove and poured himself a second cup of coffee. "Tina, I can't get a straight word out of either one of them. What the devil's been going on?" Gena asked.

Toth, Tina and Diamondback laughed.

"That's the right phrase," Tina said.

"Maybe you think it's funny"—Mrs. Scarf bristled—"but Sterling Smollett over at the dry-goods store said he won't do business with me anymore. Same for Drew at the livery stable and Perkins with his corn and grain."

"Don't worry, Mrs. Scarf," Tina said. "Word's getting around town right now about what happened. By the time you leave this office, they'll be apologizing all over themselves."

"But it's so . . . so . . ."

"Crazy?" Tina offered.

"Yes. How'd this happen to us?"

"Like any people with an unpopular belief," Diamondback answered, "they had to band together to survive. But once they came out here, they needed more land so they could bring others out."

"My land. They wanted to do those sick things on Rocking S land. That's why they killed my husband?"

"Yes. And when you didn't fold, they went to extremes to turn the town against you."

"But that little DuBoir girl. To kill her own brothers. And Dr. Goldhaven."

"That's just part of their way of thinking. There is no evil too great to get what you want."

"It does have a certain logic to it," Toth said, sketching furiously with his charcoal.

"But how did you figure it out?" she asked Cord.

"I couldn't have if it hadn't been for Dr. Goldhaven." His voice was somber. "When they'd looked for something to gag him with, they'd grabbed the first thing they saw, a piece of paper he'd been doodling on. Over and over he'd written the words we'd overheard Danny say. Abracadabra and hocus-pocus."

"Nonsense words."

"That's what we thought. At first." He paused, remembering Dr. Goldhaven, choking a lump down his throat. "But Dr. Goldhaven kept after it. We knew the words from phony magic acts, but the words had another origin. I found a book the doctor had used to research them. A book by a noted French historian, Jules Michelet, called *Satanism and Witchcraft.* Once I saw the book, I made the connection. Hocus-pocus is an abreviation of *Hoc est corpus meum,* which means 'This is my body.' It's used in the Holy Communion. But it's also used in certain Black Masses, with an inverted crucifix and the Mass said in reverse. That's why magicians use the words now."

"What about abracadabra?"

"Oddly enough, that's a medieval charm to ward off demons. Dates back to the great Roman physician, Serenus Sammonicus. Probably a composition of the Hebrew words, *Ha brachab dabarah,* which means, 'Speak the blessing.' They used to think it would protect you from illness. Sometimes they'd write it on paper and make the sick person eat it."

"But why was Danny saying it?" Gena Scarf asked.

"Well, I guess when he found out what his sister and the others had done, he couldn't take it anymore. It was the last horrible shock in a life filled with horrible shocks. The sense of guilt must have been overwhelming. In his fevered mind he was trying to renounce Satan."

Tina sighed. "Then you knew about them before we rode out there. And you didn't tell me."

"I wasn't sure. After I read the doctor's book and realized the possibilities, I knew we'd need some help. And since the citizens committee of Poisoned Well was about to lynch the most likely candidate, I persuaded Toth that I'd help him escape for something in return."

"Talk about bargaining with the devil." Toth chuckled, continuing to sketch.

"He agreed to follow Tina and me out to Providence Valley. If we didn't come out within a few minutes, he was to come in after us."

"And I did too," Toth proclaimed proudly. "I saved your soon-to-be-naked ass. So we're even on that lynching score."

"We're even," Cord agreed.

"What about the rest of them," Gena asked. "I mean, they've got kids and everything."

"That's up to the courts," Tina said. "I've wired for an army escort to take them to the capital. Let them figure it all out. But I'd guess the kids will be looked after, probably placed in other homes. I hope it's not too late for them."

Gena Scarf frowned. "I just can't believe Lilith DuBoir did all of what you described. She just looked like such an innocent, almost dull girl."

"Her name should have tipped me," Cord said. "In Zorastrianism Lilith is a female night demon."

"Where do you get all that stuff, Diamondback." Toth shook his head. "It's spooky."

Cord smiled. "Things interest me."

Judgement at Poisoned Well

"Well, then," Mrs. Scarf said, standing up. "I guess that settles that. I still have my land, and there's still not going to be any barbed wire keeping my cattle from grazing."

"For now," Tina warned. "But the land will probably go up for sale again, and whoever buys it will more than likely be using barbed wire too. It's just the way things are now."

"Maybe so." Mrs. Scarf smiled icily. "But in the meantime I can try to raise the money to buy the land myself." She walked toward the front door, hesitated. "Can I speak to you a moment, Mr. Diamondback?"

Cord followed her out the front door. She closed it behind her. Her flat blue eyes glinted like the sun off a frozen lake. "I understand you might be available to work out a lease contract in the event someone else buys the land over in Providence Valley?"

"I have a few ideas."

"Well, I've had quite a ride today and feel a little grimy. I've decided to take a room at the Deerlodge, maybe get me a bath. Perhaps we can discuss the matter further there." She didn't wait for a reply, but sauntered off toward the hotel. Diamondback watched her swiveling hips appreciatively for a few seconds before going back inside. Before he could close the door, Tina was nudging him back outside. She pulled the door closed behind her.

"Dave's coming back tomorrow," she said. "I got a wire an hour ago."

"You look happy."

"I am, Cord. Once he gets back I'm never letting him leave here again."

"What about your badge? You turning that in?"

She looked down, embarrassed. "I know I said I would. But I've decided not to. He's been after the town council to authorize funds for a deputy, and I'm gonna do my damnedest to convince them I'm right for the job."

"After what's happened, I don't think they'll take much convincing."

"That's what I'm hoping." She looked down again, flipped her hair over her shoulder. "The thing is, my house is just down the street there." She pointed in the opposite direction of the Deerlodge Hotel. "I've got a few things to do around the house. Some cleaning. Cooking. I figure to be working all afternoon, depending on how long my leg holds out."

"And you could use some help?"

"I wouldn't mind." She winked, limping off down the street, her long black hair bouncing to her waist.

The door opened and Duncan Toth stepped out, sketch pad under his arm.

"Hey, what's going on? I was getting lonely in there."

Cord said nothing.

"Well, I'm off to California. Some nasty business going on there between some rival logging companies." Toth took a few steps, stopped, turned around. "Oh, I almost forgot. Here's another Toth original for your collection. They're a wise investment, you know?" He handed over the drawing, but when Cord took hold, Toth didn't let go. His face was intent, serious. "I just want to keep things straight, Diamondback. Just because we evened out here, that doesn't square us. I still owe you for my temporary retirement. Understand?"

"Understand."

Toth nodded, released the drawing and smiled grandly. Then he spun around and walked away, chuckling.

Cord looked at the drawing. The skill and style were unmistakable, but the subject matter was quite different from the others. It was an erotic sketch, just short of being lewd. A woman's legs were wrapped around Cord's naked back. Her face was hidden in the shadows so he couldn't tell if it was meant to be Gena Scarf or Tina Jennings. But what caught Cord's eye was the strange pattern of shadows that crisscrossed his image's back. They fell in the same distinctive pattern as his secret scars. Coincidence? But they were only meant to be shadows . . . weren't they?

Cord stood in front of the sheriff's office and glanced down the street where Toth had disappeared. He looked over at the Deerlodge Hotel where Mrs. Scarf was preparing her bath. He looked in the opposite direction, where Tina Jennings was alone in her house, waiting.

Diamondback took a deep breath and started walking.

More bestselling western adventure from Pinnacle, America's #1 series publisher.
Over 8 million copies of EDGE in print!

- ☐ 41-279-7 Loner #1 — $1.75
- ☐ 41-868-X Ten Grand #2 — $1.95
- ☐ 41-769-1 Apache Death #3 — $1.95
- ☐ 41-282-7 Killer's Breed #4 — $1.75
- ☐ 41-836-1 Blood on Silver #5 — $1.95
- ☐ 41-770-5 Red River #6 — $1.95
- ☐ 41-285-1 California Kill #7 — $1.75
- ☐ 41-286-X Hell's Seven #8 — $1.75
- ☐ 41-287-8 Bloody Summer #9 — $1.75
- ☐ 41-771-3 Black Vengeance #10 — $1.95
- ☐ 41-289-4 Sioux Uprising #11 — $1.75
- ☐ 41-290-8 Death's Bounty #12 — $1.75
- ☐ 41-772-1 Tiger's Gold #14 — $1.95
- ☐ 41-293-2 Paradise Loses #15 — $1.75
- ☐ 41-294-0 Final Shot #16 — $1.75
- ☐ 41-838-8 Vengeance Valley #17 — $1.95
- ☐ 41-773-X Ten Tombstones #18 — $1.95
- ☐ 41-297-5 Ashes and Dust #19 — $1.75
- ☐ 41-774-8 Sullivan's Law #20 — $1.95
- ☐ 40-487-5 Slaughter Road #22 — $1.50
- ☐ 41-302-5 Slaughterday #24 — $1.75
- ☐ 41-802-7 Violence Trail #25 — $1.95
- ☐ 41-837-X Savage Dawn #26 — $1.95
- ☐ 41-309-2 Death Drive #27 — $1.75
- ☐ 40-204-X Eve of Evil #28 — $1.50
- ☐ 41-775-6 The Living, The Dying, and The Dead #29 — $1.95
- ☐ 41-312-2 Towering Nightmare #30 — $1.75
- ☐ 41-313-0 Guilty Ones #31 — $1.75
- ☐ 41-314-9 Frightened Gun #32 — $1.75
- ☐ 41-315-7 Red Fury #33 — $1.75
- ☐ 41-987-2 A Ride in the Sun #34 — $1.9
- ☐ 41-776-4 Death Deal #35 — $1.9
- ☐ 41-448-X Vengeance at Ventura #37 — $1.75
- ☐ 41-449-8 Massacre Mission #38 — $1.95
- ☐ 41-450-1 The Prisoners #39 — $1.9
- ☐ 41-451-X Montana Melodrama #40 — $2.2
- ☐ 41-924-4 The Killing Claim #41 — $2.2
- ☐ 41-106-5 Two of a Kind — $1.75
- ☐ 41-894-9 Edge Meets Steele: Matching Pair — $2.2

Buy them at your local bookstore or use this handy coupon
Clip and mail this page with your order

**PINNACLE BOOKS, INC.—Reader Service Dept.
1430 Broadway, New York, NY 10018**

Please send me the book(s) I have checked above. I am enclosing $_____ (please add 75¢ to cover postage and handling). Send check or money order only—no cash or C.O.D.'s.

Mr./Mrs./Miss _____

Address _____

City _____ State/Zip _____

Please allow six weeks for delivery. Prices subject to change without notice.